BOOK FOUR

THE FAE REALM SERIES

CATHLIN SHAHRIARY

For Kristann, my sister and best friend. I love you!

For Jo, the Boss Bean, who would have loved Callie's story if she had lived to read it.

PROLOGUE

Six months earlier

CALLIE COULD BARELY process how quickly her life had just changed. Could it be only a week ago that all she was worried about was midterm exams and boys? It felt like a lifetime. Never in her wildest dreams would she have imagined Fae were real and her best friend, Ianthe, was half Fae, let alone that the guy Callie had fallen for was a Fae who would kidnap her in some twisted revenge plot for his brother's death, but that was what had happened. She knew from this moment on her life would never be the same.

She shot a final glance at the boy—*not boy*, she had to remind herself, *Fae*—the Fae who had held her captive. Evin's honey-colored eyes met hers, and as much as she tried to fight the pull, she felt it. *Must be Stockholm syndrome*, she thought as she tore her gaze from his, but not before seeing the longing and regret on his face. His shoulders slumped forward as he walked out the door.

It wasn't that he'd been cruel to her—he'd been incredibly kind—but the fact remained that he had lied to her and taken her into a world of danger in order to use her. She couldn't stand to be used. Her parents used her all the time as a pawn in their divorce, and it drove her crazy. She'd had friends use her at her old school, and boys tried to use her, too. The one time she'd thought things would be different... She sighed. It was no use. He was no different than the others; if only her heart would believe it.

Conall paused as he passed by her, leaning in close. "For what's it worth, I think he'll regret it for the rest of his life—and for us, that's a very long time." Her eyes met his emerald gaze, and stupid hope fluttered in her chest. He smiled sadly. "He really does care about you, Callie." He patted her shoulder before walking away. She cursed him for saying the exact thing she wanted to hear and cursed her heart for wanting to hear it.

She glanced once more at the closing door. It didn't matter; none of it did. They were from different worlds— literally—and she would never fit into his. This was all for the best. They could never be together. Now, if only she could convince her heart that was true.

CHAPTER 1

THE BELL RANG, indicating the end of the day. *Just two more weeks until freedom*, she thought. As much as she yearned for the end of high school, a part of her was a little sad. Her senior year hadn't been that bad, kidnapping excluded. She'd made a friend she knew would last a lifetime, experienced the sweet satisfaction of watching popular mean girls' jaws drop when Conall enrolled in school on Ianthe's arm, went to a few dances, went on a few dates (including one to prom), and got a partial scholarship to her first-choice school. Of course, there were a few hiccups along the way—a forced Christmas with Dad, Mom's new boyfriend (now thankfully her ex) who was a dick, and the general feeling that something was missing and she wasn't quite whole without it. *When you give your heart to someone, does it ever come back whole?*

"Cal!" Ianthe's voice cut through the din as she walked down the hall. Leaning against her locker with her arms crossed, Ianthe stood tapping her foot impatiently. "Let's go!" she begged in a whiny tone.

"Where's your boy toy?" Callie teased.

"If you're referring to Conall, he started drivers ed classes today." Ianthe smirked.

Callie giggled. "And when he applies to get his license, how is he going to explain his age?"

Ianthe rolled her eyes and dropped her voice to a whisper. "Believe it or not, he has a birth certificate and a Social Security card. They're forged, of course, but I was rather surprised to discover Fae are resourceful enough to think about documentation in the human world."

"But not resourceful enough to drive cars." Callie chuckled, opening her locker and tugging her books out of her bag, thankful her teachers had ceased giving her homework and the only thing she had left to do was study for finals.

"Yeah, well, for some reason most Fae and technology just don't mix. I'm not sure if it's their backward ideas or something to do with their magic, or perhaps all the old folklore about Fae and iron is true. Plus, you've been over there—it's like stepping back into the Middle Ages. Well, at least the Unseelie territory was like that. The first time I was there, I expected everything to be lit by candles and was surprised they had some sort of magic that acted like electricity, although I'm pretty sure the kitchen still used fire to cook their food. The Seelie, on the other hand, seemed to be a little more advanced, more like the Victorian era if I had to describe it."

"Yeah, the only places I saw were the forest and"—she swallowed—"he-who-shall-not-be-named's house." She zipped up her bag, fighting the turbulent emotions that always resurfaced at the mention or thought of Evin.

"Cal."

"What?" She slammed the locker closed, afraid of where this conversation was headed.

"It's been months now…don't you think it's time for us to be able to say his name?"

"No, and as my BFF, you should support me."

"True, but also as your BFF, I should call you out on your bullshit." Ianthe sighed. "I know you don't want to hear this, but it's almost summer and we'll be leaving for college soon, so I think it needs to be said. I know what Evin did was wrong."

Callie flinched at his name, but Ianthe pushed on, ripping the Band-Aid off.

"But I talked to him in his dream. I saw him in tears over his decision to take you. I saw the regret in his eyes, and when you guys came to rescue me from Casimir, his eyes never left you. He was heartbroken, too. Don't you think…" She twisted the strap of her backpack. "Don't you think you both have suffered enough?" Her voice softened at the end, knowing what a blow this would be.

Callie staggered, her back hitting her locker. "Are you suggesting I *forgive* him?" The betrayal stung. Her best friend knew how much he'd hurt her, how much his deception had broken her heart.

"I'm just saying maybe you're not the only one who's miserable, and maybe if you'd let go of a little bit of your pride and anger, you could see there's a simple way to end your misery."

"He kidnapped me. He *lied* to me."

Ianthe knew the lying part was what was holding Callie back. Sure, the kidnapping sounded bad, but it wasn't personal. The lying, however, Callie definitely had a problem with. It originated in the fact that her father was a liar. He had lied to her mother until he felt guilty enough to confess he had been having an affair with a much younger woman for a while and she was now pregnant with his child. Her mother had been devastated, her family ripped apart—not that everything had been cupcakes and rainbows before. She'd felt her father's absence in the year before he came clean, almost as if he was already emotionally distancing himself from his family, always claiming work-related excuses. Her mom had wasted no time divorcing him and moving them away. The worst part, Callie thought, was that he hadn't even fought for them. He hadn't fought to keep his kids in the same state, almost as if he were glad to be released of the burden of them holding him back from his new life and the new family he was building.

Callie was old enough to understand the ugliness that can exist in this world, but her heart had broken watching her younger brother come to terms with it all. To top it all off, the other woman had known all about them and had emailed Callie a few weeks ago, attempting to "mend the relationship with her father"—her words, not Callie's—as if wounds that big could be closed with a Band-Aid. There was no amount of frozen yogurt and junk food that could cheer her up for days after that email.

"I know, I just…I just want to see you happy again, that's all. I'm worried about you."

"I'll be fine, Thee." Callie bent down and grasped her backpack, slinging it over her shoulder. "Besides, it's not like it would have worked out. You know there's still the whole I'm human and he's Fae issue."

"But if you love him—" she protested.

Callie threw her hand up. "Do I love him? Honestly, I don't know. We weren't together all that long, and sure I started falling for who he was pretending to be, but now I have no clue what was real and what wasn't." She gave her best friend a pointed look before her next statement. "Besides, we both know sometimes love just isn't enough." She heard Ianthe's sharp inhalation and instantly regretted the words. It wasn't fair to remind her of what had happened to her mother. Callie turned and walked away, feeling guilty and knowing by the way Ianthe trailed behind she'd already forgiven her for lashing out.

Ianthe sighed, ignoring Callie's subtle jab and let the topic drop for now. She had said her piece and pushed her far enough. She was tired of seeing Callie plastering on a fake smile and pretending she wasn't in pain when she knew she was, especially when she knew from Conall that any time Evin contacted him, he always found a way to ask about Callie. She felt so keenly in her heart that Callie and Evin belonged together, needed each other, but perhaps Callie was right. She already knew human and Fae relationships didn't work because of her mom's affair with her father and the way Conall's mother treated his father. She would just have to let it go.

Callie pushed the front door of the school open. "Besides, I'm leaving for college in a few months, and I'm sure it will be full of available hotties."

Ianthe's elbow caught Callie's side in a quick jab. "You mean like the available hottie right over there." She smirked and nodded her head toward a guy who was leaning against his car door with his nose in a textbook. "Hey Jordan!" she called out as she waved.

Callie grabbed her hand and tugged it down "What are you doing?" she hissed.

"Thank me later," Ianthe told her, shaking off Callie's hand and skipping down the front steps to where Jordan was now studying them curiously.

He pulled a pencil from behind his ear and placed it in his textbook to mark the page before closing it. "Uh, hey Lo…I mean Ianthe." He coughed.

Ianthe smiled. She knew sometimes it was hard for the classmates she'd known for so long to switch from calling her Lola to Ianthe, but Jordan had been making an effort this year. She'd first met him when he was just a gangly preteen in middle school and his family had moved to their sleepy town from Atlanta. He'd always been rather quiet, and even though he was a star on the basketball court, he never wanted to be popular, preferring the company of books to that of people.

Callie had AP English with Jordan, and while she found his dark skin, muscular frame, and kind brown eyes nice to look at, she was even more attracted to his brain. He was brilliant and observant but never seemed to pass judgment on others. He was an enigma, destroying all high school stereotypes. He was revered by the brains for his smarts, respected by the jocks for his skills on the court, and pursued by cheerleaders but determined to be single after his girlfriend moved away the summer before senior year.

"Were you getting in some last-minute cramming?" Ianthe asked.

"One can never be too prepared," Jordan replied.

"Congratulations on your scholarship by the way." Ianthe's voice broke through Callie's thoughts. "Did you know Callie is also going to CU Boulder?"

His eyes widened slightly, and a smile spread across his face. "Really?"

Ianthe's elbow once again found her side, and she took the hint. "Yep. It was my safety."

"Your safety?" The corners of his lips turned down.

Callie sighed. "Yeah, I got into my first choice, but unfortunately I couldn't make things work to go to NYU. I thought..." She swallowed. "I thought my parents would be able to help more than they could." Disappointment in her father's refusal to fund her dream school seeped through her veins. Her mom and grandma had tried to convince her to go, said they would find some way to make it work, but she didn't like the idea of them getting buried under loans.

He smiled sadly. "I get it. I'd probably be at a community college if I hadn't received a full ride." His eyes brightened. "Well, it will be nice to have a friendly face in Boulder."

"Yeah, it will." She smiled, elbowing Ianthe. "Now, if we could only get someone else to join us."

Ianthe chuckled. "I'm not going to apologize for wanting to go to a liberal arts college. Besides, it's not like I'm going to be far away—Colorado Springs is only an hour and a half from Boulder."

"But that's an hour and a half too far," Callie whined.

Ianthe rolled her eyes. "Whatever. We'd be even worse off if you were going to NYU."

"And there's the plus side of going to my second choice."

"Well, that and apparently Jordan being there with you," Ianthe added, tilting her head toward Jordan, who had been silently watching their interaction with rapt attention.

His cheeks colored slightly when Callie swung her gaze back to him. "Very true. A second positive." She didn't want to admit having a familiar face around in a new place was a comforting idea, especially someone as kind as him, someone she knew would be friendly and would help her out if she needed it.

"Maybe you guys should exchange numbers so you can contact each other when you get there." Ianthe blinked at them both innocently. Callie cut her a sharp look, thinking Jordan would for sure see how obvious Ianthe was being.

He coughed softly. "That's a great idea." He put his book down on the hood of his car and fished in his pocket for his phone, holding it out to her. Callie entered her contact information and handed it back to him. Her phone dinged a moment later, and he said, "There, now you have mine as well."

"Cool, thanks."

"Well, we should go. I have to pick up Conall soon," Ianthe replied, saving them both from any awkward silence.

"See you tomorrow," Callie added.

"See ya." Jordan gave a sort of half wave before reopening his textbook.

Ianthe pressed her lips together, forcing herself to wait until they got into the car to gush over the exchange. The minute the door closed and Callie sat down in the passenger seat, she squealed. "Oh my god! You got Jordan's number!"

"Geez, calm down. It doesn't mean I'm going to use it. Besides, what's with the 180? Weren't you just trying to convince me to give a certain someone else another chance?"

"Well, yeah, but I just want to see you happy, and Jordan's a great guy. He's one of the few people who's always been nice to me, even after all that mess that happened last year. He's actually the reason I'm still graduating on time. He helped me get caught up and tutored me when I needed it after rehab, and he never once judged me for it. He just let me know he was there if I needed to talk about anything. There should be more guys like him."

"Geez, Thee, maybe you should date him then."

Ianthe shoved her playfully before starting the car and pulling out of the school parking lot. "Don't be silly. I already have a guy, but you, my friend, are as free as a bird."

"So, what do you need to study for tonight?" Callie asked, changing the subject.

"Bio. You?"

"Just need to prep for my final presentation in English. You know, at my old school, you didn't have to take the finals if you had above a certain grade."

"Damn, that must be nice. Wish our teachers did that."

"It was nice. Oh well, at least there's only a few left and then graduation!"

"Do you have to go see your dad in July?"

"Nope. I used my new job and working to save money for college as my excuse. I do feel a little bad sending Sean off to visit him on his own, but there's not much I can do to protect him when I'll be leaving for college in the fall anyway."

"He'll be okay. He's a strong kid."

"What about you? Did you guys make a decision about going to spend some time with Grace?"

"We did. We decided it would probably be best if we all took a family vacation instead, so Aunt Grace will be joining me, Dad, and Conall for my graduation trip to Orlando. Harry Potter World, here we come!"

"Man, I'm so jealous."

Ianthe stuck out her bottom lip. "You know you can still come with us if you want." She added some puppy dog eyes in an attempt to persuade Callie to say yes.

"You know I'd love to, but I can't afford it, and there's no way I'm letting you guys pay for it."

"But my dad already offered to pay as your graduation present."

"I know, and you know how I feel about handouts. I'd feel guilty the whole trip, and that's no way to feel when you're at the most magical place on Earth."

"I thought that was Disneyland?"

"Psh, that was before Harry Potter. It's all about magic. Disney ain't got nothing on HP."

"Spoken like a true Potterhead."

"Hufflepuff for life."

"Come on, you know Gryffindor is what it's all about."

"Hmm...what house do you think Conall would fall in?"

Ianthe squealed. "Oh my god! I can't believe I haven't had him sorted yet. I'll let you know later tonight," she replied with a saucy wink.

CHAPTER 2

WHEN CALLIE WALKED into school the next morning, still chuckling over the text Ianthe had sent her late last night with GRYFFINDOR in all caps, the hallways were full of chatter and people whispering. She wondered who the current victim of the gossip mill was, breathing a sigh of relief when no one's eyes followed her. She stopped by Ianthe's locker first, spotting her and Conall whispering furiously back and forth, and for a moment she paused, unsure if she should proceed. Their faces didn't have the starry-eyed, love-struck expressions they normally did when they were caught whispering to each other. Instead, Ianthe's face was slightly pale and her eyes were wide, while Conall looked grim. Ianthe's violet gaze spotted her, so she continued toward them.

"Hey guys, what's up?"

"Did you see the news last night?"

"Come on, you know the only news I watch is *The Daily Show*, and I only watch that for the laughs and the eye candy." She fluttered her eyes closed. "Mmm, Trevor

Noah." She opened her eyes again, anticipating their normal banter, but Ianthe's usually playful smile was absent.

"So, you haven't heard what happened to Mr. Norris?"

"The owner of the convenience store on the corner?" Callie asked.

Ianthe nodded.

"Nope, and apparently I may be the only one with the way everyone else is abuzz this morning—unless there's something more scandalous I'm also missing out on."

Ianthe shook her head.

Callie had liked Mr. Norris. She smiled remembering the first time she stopped in at his little store with Ianthe.

The little old man behind the counter smiled widely the minute they walked through the door.

"Well, look who's here! Going back to your roots I see." He motioned toward her hair and winked at his own pun.

"Yeah, yeah. Save it, old man—I'm taken." She smiled affectionately at him in return. "This is Callie. She just moved here a few weeks ago."

"Nice to meet you, Callie, and look at that red hair." He whistled. "My Jo, she had red hair, and what a beaut' she was with a fiery spirit to match. She's been gone two years now, and not a day goes by that I don't miss her." His voice trailed off, lost in a memory while they wandered over to the back and filled up two slushie cups.

When they approached the counter to pay, he picked right back up where he'd left off. "I bet you're a little spitfire just like my Jo."

Ianthe roared with laughter. "You have no idea, Mr.

Norris. No idea."

Callie elbowed her playfully in return then blinked up at Mr. Norris with her best impression of innocent doe eyes. "I don't know what she's talking about. I'm an angel."

The laugh that left his mouth was loud and booming, straight from his belly. "Oh, my wife would have loved you." He waved them off when they tried to pay. "My treat, as long as you come back by and visit me sometime."

From then on, he would light up whenever she stopped in, and he would always tell her never to change her hair color, saying she'd find a boy who would appreciate her fiery spirit.

"Is he okay?" She asked the question even though she already knew the answer, could read it in their eyes. She sighed when they didn't respond. "Well, at least he's with his Jo now." The first bell rang, cutting off their conversation. "Crap, I still need to swing by my locker. Catch you in Spanish?"

Ianthe nodded in reply.

She dashed to her locker, grabbing what she needed for calculus, and barely made it to her seat before the tardy bell rang. She tried to focus on class, knowing her final was days away, but she couldn't help but overhear snippets of conversation.

"…attacked…"

"I can't believe it."

"Bryce said…"

"Do you think it was rabid?"

The pattern continued in other classes. When she asked Ianthe about it in Spanish, her friend put up a finger and mouthed, "Lunch," before turning her attention back to the teacher.

Thankfully lunch was next on her schedule so she wouldn't have to wait too long to get the whole story, but she knew from what she had overheard that poor Mr. Norris hadn't died peacefully in his sleep of old age like she had hoped.

She grabbed her tray and made her way to their normal table outside. Ianthe and Conall were both there already since Ianthe usually brought them both lunch from home.

"Okay, spill it. I've been hearing some crazy shit all morning." She picked up her slice of pizza and took a large bite.

"I would've told you earlier if the bell hadn't rung." Ianthe's eyes held an apology, but Callie wasn't sure what she was apologizing for—not having a chance to tell her earlier or what she was about to reveal. A glance at Conall's hard expression was all it took to know this was a conversation none of them wanted to have.

"He was attacked last night outside of his gas station. Apparently, Bryce found him when he stopped for gas around 2 AM."

The way she carefully worded each phrase and paused let Callie know whatever Bryce had found was not a scene anyone would wish to stumble across.

Ianthe swallowed hard before continuing. "The official report said he was attacked by some sort of large animal."

Callie glanced over to the popular table where she could see a bigger than normal crowd gathered around Bryce, who was animatedly describing what he'd seen. She saw him drag his hand across his center, his fingers rounded like claws, and then he flipped both of his hands out in front of his stomach, his every motion indicating that poor Mr. Norris had been gutted. She glanced at the slice of pizza in her hand and set it back on her tray, no longer hungry.

"There was evidence of claw and teeth marks." Ianthe swallowed again and drew in a deep breath.

"So, what kind of large animal are we talking about? Bear? Mountain lion?"

"The report says 'unknown'. We think they ruled both of those animals out," Conall responded.

"And how do you know what the official report says?"

"I may have paid a visit to the coroner's office this morning and persuaded them to let me look at it." He smirked.

Ianthe snorted. "He means he used his magic to access the information."

The hair on the back of Callie's neck rose. She remembered the sensation of Conall using his powers to manipulate her own emotions. Of course, he had just been trying to calm her down at the time, but she knew he could be extremely effective. She swallowed the rising sense of dread resting in her belly. She knew what it meant that he was investigating this. Bear and mountain lion attacks were rare, and she knew only one thing would make Conall this interested in poor Mr. Norris' attack. "Do you think it was a Fae?"

Conall's Adam's apple bobbed. "Not a Fae, but I can think of a few creatures in the realm that could be responsible."

"Creatures? There are creatures in Fae?"

Conall snorted. "Of course, just as you have animals here. Ours are like yours in many ways. Some are harmless, and others you wouldn't want to come across un-armed, especially if they are hungry."

"But if they're in Fae, how did one get here?"

"That is exactly what I intend to find out," Conall re-plied, his green eyes sparkling with something otherworld-ly. Other people might not have noticed it, but Callie had begun to see when his glamour slipped, usually only when he was driven by extreme emotions like the night they res-cued Ianthe from Casimir. As on that night, in this moment she could see a hint of the Unseelie urges he kept in check, a glimmer of something dark and wild in his eyes, some-thing that craved violence and was excited by the prospect of a hunt. A chill ran down her spine, her mouth suddenly dry.

Ianthe put her hand on his knee and squeezed, his eyes returning to normal the instant he felt her touch. It was eerie. Callie had come to know Conall, how sweet and de-voted he was to her bestie. He was a genuinely good soul, so much so that she would sometimes forget he wasn't en-tirely human. She wondered what it would be like to have that darkness living under her skin.

Does Evin ever feel that way? Do the Seelie have the same cravings? She shook her head, trying to rid her mind of the thoughts of him that seemed to slip in unexpectedly and always left her feeling a little empty.

"...wasn't the first." Ianthe's voice yanked her back to the present.

"What was that?"

"We don't think Mr. Norris was the first victim." She sighed. "When Conall was talking to the coroner, he said a female hiker was brought in two weeks ago with the same injuries."

Callie blanched, and Conall reached over to pat her hand reassuringly. "Don't worry, Callie. I'll find whatever it is, and I'll take care of it. In the meantime, just make sure you're cautious and always aware of your surroundings when you're out, especially at night."

"Well, it's a good thing I start my first shift at Yogurt Land tonight, isn't it?" she joked, but it fell flat, and Ianthe frowned. "It'll be fine, Thee. It's not like I'll be there alone. It's just training tonight. Don't worry," Callie told her reassuringly.

She nodded. "If you need us, if something feels off, just call, okay?"

"Will do, boo, but now it's time for English." Just as soon as she said it, the bell rang, signaling the end of lunch. She picked up her tray of mostly uneaten food and tossed it in the trash.

"Say hi to Jordan for me," Ianthe called after her, trying to lighten the bomb that had just been dropped. Callie responded in typical fashion with a one-finger salute over her shoulder.

Her stomach churned. A creature from the Fae realm was loose in her town, and no one knew who it would hurt next.

CHAPTER 3

"SO, YOU JUST weigh the yogurt and then ring them up. Pretty easy." His voice cracked on the word easy, and she fought the urge to cringe. It was rather embarrassing to have someone younger training her, especially when that someone was a tall, gangly sophomore whose voice was still going through puberty. It wouldn't have been so bad if Steve were actually nice, but the kid had done nothing but treat her like an idiot since she started training with him an hour earlier. "Do you need me to show you again?" He raised one condescending eyebrow, his lack of patience evident in his tone.

"Nope, I think I got it. Thanks."

He snorted in reply, which increased her desire to prove him wrong. She knew this was her first job and everyone had to start somewhere. She hadn't needed to work before, but with college and all the expenses that came along with it looming in the distance, it was time. She just hoped not all her shifts would be spent with Steve. Perhaps there were some nicer staff members; otherwise it was definitely not going to be as fun as she'd thought.

She glanced over at the people milling around eating their yogurt. There was an older couple seated at a familiar table holding hands. It didn't seem like that long ago she had sat at that same table excitedly introducing Ianthe to her new boyfriend. She cringed, remembering how stupid she had been to believe him, how easily she'd fallen for every line, how he had even lied about his name.

"Sorry I'm late," a shorter girl with bubblegum pink hair announced as the bell tinkled behind her. Callie took in her matching uniform and a small amount of ink peeking out from under her left sleeve.

Steve grunted and nodded his head. "Vicki, glad you could make it. You're lucky George isn't around today."

"Ain't that the truth, but you won't report me, will ya, Stevie?" She batted the lashes of her heavily lined blue eyes up at him.

"Not this time, but let's not make it a habit. Think you can help the newb for a bit? I've been waiting to take my break."

"Sure, of course. Go enjoy your fifteen minutes of freedom."

Steve snorted again and walked off toward the back. A customer cleared his throat, drawing Callie's attention back toward the register. "Oh, hello. Sorry about that." He placed his tub of frozen yogurt on the scale. "Will that be all for you?" she asked.

"Yes, thanks."

She tapped the buttons on the screen as Steve had shown her. "That will be $5.83 please."

He handed her his credit card and she stood there for a second, scanning the options on the screen, unsure what to do next. Steve hadn't shown her how to actually accept payments.

The pink-haired girl appeared over her shoulder. "It's the bottom left," she whispered.

"Thanks," Callie replied, pressing the button and then swiping the card.

"We're due to get a chip reader next week so I'm sure we'll have some kind of mandatory training about it, but for now that will do the trick." She smiled warmly.

"Would you like your receipt?" Callie asked the customer. He shook his head and she handed back his card, turning her attention to her new coworker. "Hey, I'm Callie—the newb, apparently."

"Vicki," the pink-haired girl replied, holding out her hand to shake.

Callie noted her firm handshake and the glittery mermaid-colored nails. "I like your nails."

"Thanks! Just got them done, which is why I was a little late." She winked, wiggling her fingers out in front of her. "But if Steve asks, I had car trouble."

"So, speaking of Steve"—she glanced over her shoulder at the hallway where he had disappeared—"is he always like that?"

"Like what? A condescending ass?"

Callie laughed. "I guess that answers my question."

"Eh, Steve's all right. He's just one of those smart kids who has no patience for people who aren't as quick as he is, but once you get to know him, he grows on you. Oh, and once you meet George, you'll be glad to have Steve around. George has a Type A personality, a total micromanager who always has to find something for us to do the minute things slow down. Last week he had me scrubbing the men's restroom, and girl, let me tell you, I don't care how old they are—they can't aim worth shit."

Callie wrinkled her nose. "Gross."

Vicki twirled a pink lock around her finger. "You're telling me. My advice: never let him catch you looking at your phone. Steve, on the other hand, couldn't care less if you have your phone out as long as there aren't customers around and you're still getting your work done. So, you see, he grows on you."

The rest of her first shift passed quickly with Vicki around. Even Steve seemed a little less irritable when she proved she wasn't incompetent and could take direction well without much assistance. Overall, she would have said it was a good first shift, one of many to come—and hey, at least she could get froyo whenever she wanted.

"Come on, Callie, we can walk out to our cars together. Steve will close up. Are you parked around back?" Vicki linked her arm with Callie's, tugging her outside when she nodded in reply. "Me too!" The yogurt shop was situated on a busy road with the entrance and large windows facing the street and only a few parking spots right out front. Of course, one of the things she'd been told when she was hired was those spots were for customers only, so she would have to park in the public lot a short walk away through the alley out the back.

She shivered despite the warm air of the night. The alley hadn't seemed so ominous in the light of day, but now, knowing what could be out there in the dark, she felt another chill run through her.

"Cold?" Vicki asked.

"No, just thinking about the animal attack last night."

"Oh yeah, I heard about that." She paused and looked around dramatically then giggled, pulling Callie forward. "We're in the middle of the town. Ain't no animal going to venture this far in, especially on a busy street like this. Don't worry. We'll be fine," Vicki said confidently, not the least bit concerned.

Still, Callie kept her gaze alert, scanning their surroundings as she approached her beat-up, red Chevy Cavalier.

"I'm over here." Vicki jerked her head toward an older, baby blue VW beetle. "You on tomorrow?"

Callie shook her head. "Friday night."

"Perfect! I close Friday too. I'll see you then!" She gave Callie a quick hug before bouncing over to her car.

Callie unlocked her doors and plugged her phone into the charger, watching as Vicki pulled out and drove away. She turned the key once, her car making a sort of coughing sound but not turning over. She rubbed the dash. She knew she needed to take her car in, but things like that took money, which neither she nor her mom had—one of the many reasons she had been eager to start a job before school was officially done. She knew if she asked, her dad would give her some cash to fix the vehicle, but there was no way she was ever going to ask him for it.

She sighed. "Come on, girl. You can do it. I know you can. You've still got some life in you," she cooed, rubbing her hand across the steering wheel in a caress. She turned the key again and the engine caught this time. "That's my girl."

As she was pulling into her driveway, her phone dinged with a text. She parked her car and turned the engine off before reaching over for her phone. She was pleasantly surprised to see Jordan's number on the screen.

Jordan: Hey, Callie. You all set
for your presentation tomorrow?

She blushed, typing her response. She still had a few things she needed to make sure were in order since the presentation was a major part of their final grade. Her English teacher didn't believe in finals, instead having each student select an author to read and research, presenting an analysis of their work. She'd actually enjoyed the project and had learned a lot about one of her favorite authors, George Sand, a female French author from the 1800s who wrote under a man's name and challenged societal expectations of women both in her private life and in her writing. Callie had fallen in love with her writing when she read *Indiana* and became even more enthralled as she dug into her research. She was eager to give her presentation and knew her class would eat it up. The woman had cross-dressed and carried on multiple affairs with both men and women, all incredibly scandalous, especially given the culture of the time period.

Callie: I think so. When's yours
again?

She unclicked her seatbelt and unplugged her phone.

Jordan: Monday

She collected her purse and climbed out of her car, making sure to hit the lock button on her way out. She moved on autopilot, her attention on her phone, thinking of what she should reply next to keep the conversation going. She heard a dog bark like mad in the distance, causing her heart to skip a beat. It was only then that she remembered what might lurk in the shadows and quickened her pace until she was safely inside her house with the door locked.

"How was your first day at work?" her grandmother asked, popping out of the kitchen with an eager smile.

Callie released a deep breath, her heart rate returning to normal. She smiled as she walked toward the kitchen. "It was just oh so thrilling, Grams. I mean, learning how to weigh cups of frozen yogurt and swipe credit cards—I just didn't think I would *ever* get it right."

Her grandmother swatted her with a hand towel when she got close enough. "Any more sass and I'll just let your brother polish off the plate we saved for you. He's been eyeing it for quite some time now."

She considered her options as she followed her grandmother into the kitchen. "What is it?"

"Spaghetti and meatballs." Grams retrieved a plate wrapped in foil from the oven.

Callie smiled sweetly. "Work was fine. My shift supervisor was a bit of a jerk, thinks we're all idiots, but I met this girl Vicki who seems really nice."

"There, was that so hard?" She placed the plate on the counter and Callie pulled a stool over. "Milk or water?"

"Water please."

Her grandmother got her a glass of ice water and a fork, and Callie dug in. It was heaven. Her grandmother was Italian and could cook like nobody's business, making everything from scratch, of course—none of the "canned crap", as she called it.

"Mom at work?" Callie asked between bites of food.

"Yep, until close."

Her mom had started bartending when they moved in with Grams. She also substitute taught. She claimed it was all temporary until she could get a permanent teaching

26

position, but in order to do that, there were a few things she needed to take care of to get her certificate transferred over to Colorado and get current on new teaching trends. She had taught first grade for three years before Callie was born and decided to take a few years off while Callie was young. Her dad made enough money to cover things, and it wasn't like teaching paid a whole lot, especially when you figured in daycare costs, so she had continued to be a stay-at-home mom and did some private tutoring in the evenings after Sean was born.

The last few years, she had been a part-time tutor at Sean's school, which was nice because it gave her time to be there for them after school but also kept her from being bored. Obviously, that was before Callie's dad had torn their family apart. Now her mom had no choice but to work to pay the bills, and she knew she didn't want to live in Grams' house forever. While subbing was great until she could get her paperwork in order, it wasn't always constant, and she made good tips bartending.

"And Sean?"

"He's staying the night at Logan's."

Callie was glad Sean had been able to find Logan just as she had found Ianthe. They had all made sacrifices and compromises this last year, learning to live with Grams in a new city, starting at a new school, making new friends. She loved how fierce and protective her grandmother was, and that was probably one of the only reasons she felt comfortable leaving in the fall. She knew her mom and brother would be in great hands. She finished her meal while Grams cleaned the kitchen and put dishes away.

When she was done, she rinsed her plate and loaded it into the dishwasher. "Thanks Grams." She threw her arms around her, hugging tightly.

"Any time, my Callie-kins. Any time."

She squeezed her grandmother and kissed her on the cheek. "I'm going to make sure everything's ready for my presentation. I'll see you in the morning."

"Good night, sassy pants."

Pulling her phone from her pocket, she closed her bedroom door. Still nothing from Jordan. She stared at his last message before pulling up Ianthe's number.

"What's up?"

"Jordan texted me."

Ianthe squealed. "OMG! What did he say?"

"He asked if I was ready for my presentation for English."

"That's it?" Disappointment laced her words.

"That's it, and then I asked him when his presentation is and he said Monday and now I have no freaking clue what to say to him. Ugh. Why? Why did you make me talk to him?"

Ianthe chuckled. "I didn't *make* you do anything. Please, you were crushing on him at the beginning of the year. I was merely trying to help push things along, and it looks like I did. The rest is up to you, Cal. Just be yourself. If he doesn't like you for you then he's not worth it. Don't overthink it—just type something back. You're probably killing him with suspense. Oh, and you better be ready to fill me in on all the details tomorrow! Now go text him." With that her best friend ditched her, ending the call.

She opened the text conversation.

```
Callie: How about you? Are you ready
yet or are you going to finish up
this weekend? I'm kind of glad mine
```

28

```
is this week so I can just get it
over with.
```

She hit send, hating how her text sounded a little rambling.

```
Jordan: I'm done for the most part.
I'll probably tweak a few things
this weekend though.
```

She was debating what to send next when he sent another message.

```
Jordan: All right. I'm putting my
phone on silent. Need to cram for
trig before bed. See you tomorrow.
```

Well that hadn't been nearly as bad as she'd thought it would be. She wasn't sure what it was about him that made her a little nervous. Maybe she did actually like him.

```
Callie: Good night. Good luck cram-
ming. She kept her reply nice and
simple, the less complicated the
better. She'd had complicated and
didn't think her heart could sur-
vive it again.
```

She pulled up her presentation on her computer, making a few small last-minute adjustments, and when everything was exactly as she wanted it, she called it a night and got ready for bed.

She closed her eyes, ready for sleep, for wherever her dreams would take her. Part of her yearned for the times when she visited Evin in her memories, but another part dreaded it. It didn't matter how much she tried not to think about him; she had no control over her dreams.

His hand caressed her arm, gently shaking her awake. "Callie, I need to talk to you."

She blinked her eyes open slowly. "Reid?" She yawned, and he flinched.

"Drink this please." He thrust a small glass toward her. It was then that she fully woke up, remembering she was in a strange place. She had just been dreaming of Ianthe, and they had been talking about how she could get away.

"What is it?" she asked, scooting away from him and toward the wall.

He sighed. "Just water, but it will help you feel less groggy."

"Did you...did you drug me?"

"No. Well, kind of...I guess."

Her eyes widened. "You guess?" she shrieked.

"What you drank before was a very strong wine...a special kind of wine. It's not meant for humans."

"What do you mean not meant for humans?"

He sighed again. "There are some things I need to tell you, and I'm not sure how you're going to take them, but I need you to please remember I don't want to hurt you."

"You don't want to hurt me? Oh, that's real reassuring."

He plucked the glass of water from her trembling hand. "I haven't been completely honest with you, Callie, and I'm truly sorry about that. I'm sorry about a lot of things. Do you remember when I told you about my older brother?"

She nodded, unsure where he was going with this conversation but not liking it one bit. A single word popped into her head, a memory from her dream with Ianthe: Fae. Oh shit, Ianthe had told her she was Fae and said Reid was also. The realization crashed into her and her heart picked up speed. She wondered if he could hear it. What could he do if he was Fae?

"Well, my brother Reid was murdered not too long ago."

"Wait, your brother's name was also Reid?" She decided her best tactic at that moment was to play dumb and not let him know what she already knew. There was power in knowledge.

"No. My brother's name was Reid. My name is Evin. I lied to you. I wanted to get revenge on my brother's murderer, Casimir, so I followed him. I tracked him to your world and saw that he kept a very close eye on your best friend. I think he's in love with her."

"Ianthe?" She remembered this was also part of her bestie's explanation.

"Yes. I was planning to take away the only thing he cared about, just as he took that from me, but then I noticed she has Fae guarding her for some reason, so I had to be creative. I thought maybe if I got close to you, I could find a way, and then when I didn't see one, I thought maybe she would come after you if something happened to you."

"So, you pretended to like me? You used me? You used me to get to her?" He winced each time she said the word used. She closed her eyes, imagining what the pain she was feeling in her chest might look like. An image of him holding her heart in his hand and driving needles through

31

it seemed like a pretty accurate description.

He reached for her and she backed away, trying to sink into the wall. He dropped his hands. "I'm so sorry. I didn't know then who you were. In the beginning I only saw you as a means to an end, but now, now that I know you...I don't know what I'm doing anymore. I care about you. I never thought I could feel this way about a human." Another needle pierced her heart.

"If you care about me, let me go. Let me go home, please," she begged.

"I can't do that. I'm sorry. God, I made so many mistakes, but it's too late now. I'm in too deep. There are too many consequences to go back now. The only way is to push forward. I'm sorry I have to do this. I hope someday you can forgive me." His caramel-colored eyes begged her to understand, to see how much he regretted what he had done.

"It's never too late to right a wrong, Reid—I mean Evin. I won't tell a soul about this. I promise. Just let me go."

"I can't." He sounded heartbroken and resigned at the same time. The final needle pierced her.

"Then I can't forgive you." She shoved her heartbreak down just like she had after she found out about her dad and had to hold things together to help her devastated mother. She hadn't been able to let herself fall apart then, and she couldn't let herself do so now.

Her alarm beeped, yanking her from her sleep. She rubbed her eyes and threw her hand over to her alarm to shut off the incessant noise. She hated that dream, the pain always managing to feel so fresh after she relived it. If only she could forget.

CHAPTER 4

"**SO?**" **IANTHE ASKED,** sliding up next to Callie's locker.

"Where's Conall?"

"He went ahead to class. I told him we needed some girl time. So, spill! Give me all the details. What did you text him? What did he say back?" She fired off the questions without even a breath between them.

Callie sighed. "There's not much to say. Here, see for yourself." She handed her phone over to Ianthe, embarrassed about how much she had freaked out over a simple text conversation.

"Seems friendly enough. You know, the Cal I remember from the beginning of the year wasn't this shy with guys." She nudged her with her shoulder.

"Yeah, well, what's the saying? Once bitten, twice shy." She shrugged, closing her locker.

Ianthe paled slightly.

"Everything okay, Thee? There wasn't another attack

last night, was there?"

"No, nothing like that, but you should probably know—"

The sound of the bell cut off whatever she was about to say next.

"I gotta go. I can't be late to first period again or I'll get detention. Tell me in Spanish?"

Ianthe shook her head, her lips drawn tight. "Lunch."

Callie arched an eyebrow, hesitating. If it was serious, she'd be willing to take the detention for it.

Ianthe shook her head. "Go. Don't worry." She smiled, and had it been toward anyone other than Callie, they would have thought it was reassuring, but Callie could sense it was forced.

"You sure?"

"Yes! Go!" She waved her off and turned, walking down the hall toward her first class.

Callie's morning passed in a blur. She felt off after her dream the night before, and whatever Ianthe had been about to tell her wasn't going to be pleasant. Add all that on top of the fact that she was due to give her presentation after lunch and her stomach was churning with anxiety when she grabbed her tray and headed out to find Ianthe and Conall, but they weren't there yet. She sat down and nibbled on her fries, unsure if her nerves would allow her to eat, and then her phone vibrated on the table. She tapped it, hoping it was Ianthe explaining why they were late, but was pleasantly surprised when she saw Jordan's name.

Jordan: Nervous?

Was she that obvious? She glanced around, trying to see if he was nearby, but didn't spot him, so she typed out a reply.

Callie: A little bit.

The clunk of a tray brought her attention back to the table, where Ianthe and Conall had just sat down. "Sorry, the ladies room was a little packed. What's that smile about?"

"What smile?" Callie asked, noticing that she was indeed smiling. "I can't be happy to see my bestie and her boy?"

"Certainly you can, but I have a feeling that's not the reason."

As if to prove her right, Callie's phone vibrated on the table again.

Ianthe smirked. "Who's texting you?"

"My mom," Callie replied dryly, not sure why she didn't just admit who it was.

Jordan: Don't be. You've got this!

"Last time I checked, texts from your mom didn't make you blush," Ianthe teased. "The boy staring at you from the table full of basketball players, on the other hand—he just might." She winked and nodded her head over her left shoulder.

Callie peeked and couldn't help but grin when she saw that he was indeed looking her way. She gave him a little wave, which he returned.

"Who are you waving at?" Conall turned around to look.

Ianthe slapped his shoulder lightly. "Spock, try to be a little less obvious. We don't want the poor boy to know we're talking about him."

35

"What? I just wanted to know who might be interested in our Callie, that's all." He smiled a little, but just like Ianthe's earlier expression, it looked forced.

They turned their attention back to their food. "So, what did you want to tell me?" Callie asked after eating about half of her fries.

Ianthe swallowed hard. "You have your English presentation next, right?"

"Yep."

"We'll talk about it after school."

Her stomach dropped, along with her voice. "Is it...is Casimir back?" she whispered.

Ianthe flinched and Conall's knuckles tightened around his bottle of water, denting the sides and causing the plastic to crinkle.

"No, nothing like that, so don't worry. We'll just talk about it later."

"Does it have to do with Mr. Norris' attack?"

Conall drained the rest of his water and looked at Ianthe. It seemed like they had a silent conversation with their eyes before he pursed his lips and shoved the rest of his sandwich into his mouth as if chewing would keep him from talking.

"Come on, Thee. You know you can tell me anything."

"I know, I just...I think it will be better if we wait and talk about this after school. You already have enough on your plate, and I want your focus to be on your presentation, not on anything else."

"Well, that's not the least bit reassuring," Callie mumbled.

"You know what this sandwich needs? It would be so

much better with some garlic spread," Conall stated awkwardly, trying to change the subject.

Ianthe blinked at Callie, pleading with her to let the subject drop for now.

Callie sighed. "And, pray tell, what is this garlic spread you speak of?"

"We use it on so much. It's kind of like your mayonnaise but has garlic and herbs in it."

"Like a garlic aioli?" Ianthe asked.

"If that's something like your mayonnaise with garlic and herbs in it, then yes."

"Hmm, I can probably try to make you some of that at home," Ianthe replied.

"Really?" His face lit up like a little boy.

"Well, no promises it will taste the same, but we can try to figure something out."

He leaned over and pressed a kiss on her cheek, staring at his girlfriend with so much admiration it made Callie a little green with envy. She wanted that—not Conall, specifically, but someone who would look at her like she'd hung the moon and stars.

"I should probably go to give myself a few minutes to look over everything before class."

Ianthe pulled her gaze away from Conall. "You sure?"

"Yep, but you *will* tell me whatever it is you're hiding from me after school. Promise?"

She nodded. "Yes, and good luck. I know you'll do great. Your presentation is so interesting and will raise a few eyebrows, but I'm sure that's exactly what you had in mind."

"You know me too well." Callie grabbed her bag and

dumped her food in the trash, glancing at her phone one more time and embracing the little boost of confidence Jordan's message gave her.

CHAPTER 5

"**S**O, HOW'D IT go?" Ianthe asked as she waited for Callie by her locker.

"Great!" She beamed, remembering how Jordan had given her a huge smile and a thumbs-up before and after her presentation.

"Even the Q&A part?"

"Surprisingly, yes. I mean, there were a few immature questions, but Ms. Akin shut that down pretty quickly, and it didn't hurt that Jordan brought up some really thought-provoking points, guiding part of the discussion."

"Oh, I'm sure that didn't hurt at all."

"Conall at drivers ed again?" she asked, noting his absence.

"Not today." Ianthe looked down and tugged on the strap of her backpack. Something was definitely up.

"Does this have something to do with what you need to tell me?"

"Yes."

"Okay, let me grab my stuff." She pulled out her notebook and the textbook she needed to study before closing her locker and swinging her bag over her shoulder.

"Do you work tonight?" Ianthe asked as they were exiting the school building.

"Nope. Tomorrow night and Saturday."

"Want to come over and hang out and we can talk?"

"Sure. I'll follow you there?"

"Okay." She headed off in the direction of her car.

Callie turned toward her own car then heard her name called from behind her. She spun around and saw Jordan jogging her way.

"Hey, you killed it today! You're making me up my game for Monday."

She rolled her eyes playfully. "Whatever. I'm pretty sure our salutatorian has it in the bag. Whatever you have to share with us will probably put my work to shame."

"Actually, I'm pretty sure compared to George Sand, John Steinbeck is going to be a snoozefest."

"Well, we can't all be cross-dressing bisexuals," she joked.

"If we all were, wouldn't that be the norm and thus, in comparison, make my author so much more interesting?"

"Huh, I guess you're right."

She loved how intelligent he was. In class, he enjoyed challenging popular opinions and making everyone think about things from a new perspective, and she adored being challenged.

"Well, I gotta jet. Ianthe's expecting me at her place."

She waved as she headed off, glad to see their conversation felt natural, lacking the awkwardness she'd felt when he had texted her the previous night. It would be fun to have someone else to hang out with over the summer, especially someone to bring along to things with Ianthe and Conall. Perhaps then she would feel like less of a third wheel.

She walked into Ianthe's house, not even bothering to knock. Not seeing Ianthe in the living room, she headed toward the kitchen, where she spotted her standing in front of the fridge.

"You know, Conall would have a fit if he found out you left your front door unlocked."

"Whatever. I knew you were right behind me, or you were supposed to be anyway, but it just so happens I saw someone talking to you in my rearview mirror as I pulled out of the lot." She grinned. "What did Jordan have to say?"

"Oh, he just wanted to tell me I did a great job on my presentation."

"Is that all?" She waggled her eyebrows, her violet eyes sparkling with mischievousness.

"Uh, yeah, actually."

"Damn. I thought maybe he'd ask you out on a date."

"Maybe he wants to be friends first, see how it goes," she suggested, and strangely, she didn't feel all that disappointed. The pace was good for her. Her feelings felt like they were constantly being tossed in the wind, back and forth between not being ready to date again and yearning for that companionship, for a spark of something. "Anyway, what did you want to talk about?"

"Sit," Ianthe replied, yanking two spoons out of a drawer and pointing to a seat at the island. She pulled a gallon of cookies 'n' cream ice cream from her freezer and sat down next to Callie, handing her a spoon.

"I'm not sure I want to have a conversation that involves the assistance of ice cream," Callie replied nervously.

Ianthe's expression was tentative. "I figured it couldn't hurt. Ice cream always helps."

"That's the truth. So where's Conall if he's not at drivers ed?" She dug her spoon into the ice cream and took a bite.

"He's out on official business."

Callie lifted her eyebrow and scooped up more ice cream. "Official business? I thought you were his official business. Isn't his job to basically guard you?"

"Well, yeah…" She trailed off, unsure of where to go from there, taking her own bite of ice cream as a stalling tactic—one Callie recognized.

She dropped her own spoon onto the counter. "Just spill it already. I'm a big girl. I can handle whatever it is you're afraid to tell me."

Ianthe exhaled heavily. "Evin showed up last night."

"Evin?" Callie gasped, his name like sweet poison on her tongue.

Ianthe bit her bottom lip. "Reports of the attacks made it back to the Seelie king, and he sent Evin to investigate. Apparently it's bad for business to have something unknown going around killing humans—have to keep the 'stupid humans' from figuring it out." She rolled her eyes and used air quotes as she spoke. "So, Evin came over to talk to Conall, and my dad, trying to overcompensate for the past, invited them both to dinner. I don't think I need to tell you how awkward that was. I mean it's not like they wanted to talk about the attacks right in front of my father. He would have freaked if he thought they had anything to do with Fae, may have even tried to send me away, and there is no way I'm going anywhere this close to graduation. Anyway, Evin asked for Conall's help since he's such a good tracker, and he was eager to team up since he was already planning to find the beast on his own."

Callie's pulse skittered. "So, Evin is here? In our town?"

Ianthe nodded.

"For how long?"

"Until they can locate the creature and send it back to Fae or destroy it."

"How long do you think that will take?"

"I'm not sure. Hopefully they'll be able to take care of it before it's able to attack anyone else." She reached over and grabbed Callie's hand, giving it a reassuring squeeze. "You don't have to worry. I already threatened him within an inch of his life not to come near you, so I'm sure you won't even see him."

Not seeing him—is that a good thing? A needling pain pricked her heart. God, why do I still feel this away about him? How can the mere mention of him being in town cause my heart to palpitate? Along with the ache, a stupid sliver of hope fluttered in her chest. She mentally squashed it as best she could.

"Do they know what it is yet?"

"Nope, but they're hoping to find out today. I think

they were going to see if they could use their combined powers of persuasion to get some more information." She shoved the carton closer to Callie. "More ice cream?"

Callie dug in, shoving a large spoonful into her mouth. She didn't know what she was feeling or how she was supposed to feel. Part of her wanted to run away and hide in her house to avoid even the slightest possibility of seeing him. The other part...well, the other part was what drove her to stay.

They spent the rest of the afternoon binging on *Supernatural*, and when Ianthe's dad called to say he would be home late, they ordered a pizza for dinner. They were just getting to Callie's favorite scene where Dean forgets who he is and screams at a cat when there was a knock at the door.

"Probably Conall," Ianthe muttered, getting up from the couch to answer it as Callie's heart picked up speed. A mixture of dread and hope churned through her at the possibility that Evin might be with him.

He greeted her with a quick kiss on the lips. "Oh, hey Callie," Conall said as he stepped through the doorway, spotting her peering at him over the couch. Her eyes quickly shot to the space behind him and disappointment dropped like a stone when he closed the door behind him.

"Any luck?" Ianthe asked.

"We got a bit more information, which helped us narrow down our suspicions."

"And?" Callie asked.

"And for the time being, I suggest you both be extremely cautious when you are outdoors, especially at night," he answered evasively.

"So, no luck tracking it then?" Ianthe asked.

Conall shook his head. "We'll keep trying of course." He snapped his mouth shut, realizing his mistake.

"It's okay. Callie knows he's here. I told her." Ianthe smiled weakly and shrugged.

Conall shifted an uneasy gaze between the girls, afraid he might have said the wrong thing.

"Really, it's fine. *I'm* fine," Callie reassured him.

He tipped his chin up in acknowledgment.

"Anyway, I should probably get going. It's late," Callie added.

"You sure?" Ianthe asked, her brow furrowed.

"I'll walk you out," Conall stated, his tone leaving little room for argument.

Callie grabbed her purse and gave Ianthe a quick hug before walking out the door with Conall. He opened the door for her, and she climbed into her car. He paused, holding the door, his expression pensive and unsure.

"Do you remember what I told you all those months ago?"

She swallowed. She remembered it clearly, the words he'd said that sometimes kept her up at night debating the possibilities: *He really does care about you.* She met his emerald eyes and nodded.

"You hold the reins. I know he won't seek you out because of the threats my girlfriend so lovingly delivered." He smirked. "However, should you need him, should you want to see him—you just say the word."

Her throat tightened and she swallowed the growing lump there. "Got it."

"And be careful. There's something out there, and not only would it kill Ianthe if something happened to you, I'd miss you too." He closed her door as she turned the ignition, which thankfully caught on the first try. He patted the top of her car twice before striding back inside. She pulled out of the driveway and focused her mind on driving, saving all the deep thoughts for when she got home and could process them better. She was so focused on her task that she missed the way Conall paused at the door, staring after her thoughtfully then glancing toward the strip of yard across the street where a figure took a step out of the shadows and stared at her retreating vehicle.

CHAPTER 6

EVIN WATCHED HER walk to her car, studying the way she moved. Her gorgeous red hair was pulled up into some sort of messy bun on top of her head. His hands twitched, longing to pull the strands free and run his fingers through it. He stared as Conall held her door open and yearned to be the one doing it instead, to be the guy who always opened doors for her. He wished he had a better angle, some way to see the face that haunted his every dream and spare thought. He also wished he were close enough to hear what was being said or at least read lips. His foot moved forward involuntarily as if drawn toward her, and it took all of his power to pull it back. He knew she didn't want to see him; she had told him as much the last time she'd spoken to him.

When she pulled out of the driveway and drove down the street, he stepped out of the shadows, wishing he could follow her. Ianthe's threat echoed through his mind. He hated how much he'd hurt Callie and, more than anything, wished there were a way she could forgive him. The last thing he wanted to do was cause her any more pain, so he remained in place.

His eyes met Conall's across the street. Conall nodded his head toward the door, an invitation for him to come inside, but he'd already spent enough time there. He waved his hand in a sort of sendoff salute, knowing Conall would pick up on his intentions. There wasn't much for them to discuss anyway. Conall had invited him to join them for dinner, but after seeing Callie there, he had to know that was no longer an option. Evin couldn't sit there knowing she had just been in that house, her scent still lingering in the air. It would have driven him mad.

He still had a protein bar Conall had brought him earlier. He unwrapped it, studying it curiously. He'd never had one before, but they were supposed to be nutritious. He sniffed it then hesitantly took a bite, almost spitting it back out immediately. It was chalky and sweet but lacked much flavor. "Ugh. How do humans eat these things?"

He sighed when his stomach growled, making him wish he had something better to eat as he took another bite, forcing himself to swallow. *If only I had a glass of ambrosia to wash it down.* Fae wine probably could have cured many things for him right then, but it also would have complicated his task. He needed to figure out what they were facing and how whatever this thing was had made it through the gateway. He had to stop the creature before it attacked someone else. They couldn't have the humans getting suspicious, and more attacks would reaffirm that the animal was unlike one they had ever seen before— something the Fae couldn't afford. Sure, there were stories told about Fae, but that was what the humans believed them to be—stories—and that was exactly what he needed them to keep believing.

CHAPTER 7

I T WASN'T A surprise that after the conversation with Conall, Evin managed to work his way into Callie's dreams again that night.

She remembered the first time they met. She was sitting outside her favorite local coffee shop, enjoying the cooling air of fall and working on a new song. She had the music but needed some lyrics to go with it, so she was playing around singing different options quietly until something felt right and then jotting it down in her journal. She must have been completely absorbed in her work because she was startled when she paused to take a drink, realizing someone else was sitting at her small table.

"That was beautiful." His voice was lower than those of the boys at school, more bass than baritone. His jet-black hair was medium length on top and fairly short on the sides, styled up in a bit of a swoop. His deep cara-mel-colored skin and chiseled facial features struck her as exotic, perhaps Native American, but what really took

her breath away was his eyes. They were so light brown she might have almost called them golden. Butterscotch! That's it! They reminded her of butterscotch. She'd never seen such a unique shade before.

"Uh, thanks." A blush crept up her cheeks knowing someone had been listening to her so closely. She'd known it was a possibility with her being outside the coffee shop, but sometimes she just needed a change of scenery to inspire her.

"I'm Reid." He held his hand out across the table.

She put down her guitar pick and shook his hand. "Callie." A spark of electricity tingled from her hand down to her toes. His grip was firm and lingered for longer than necessary. When he released it, he dragged his fingers slowly across her palm as he pulled his hand back, the friction sending more tingles down her spine.

He smiled like he could tell the effect he had on her.

The coffee shop faded around her, her dream morphing into a montage of happy memories—a date at the movies, hanging out at her house talking and listening to music, the first time they kissed. While the other memories seemed to flash by, this one seemed to happen in slow motion. The hypnotizing and intense way his eyes seemed to shift from chocolate to butterscotch (something she now suspected was his glamour slipping)...how he hovered over her lips, sharing her breath for a few agonizing heartbeats before finally closing those final centimeters... She was used to the tentative or overly enthusiastic and sloppy kisses of inexperienced boys. Evin, on the other hand, knew what he wanted and took it. He dominated her mouth in a way that left her breathless and aching for more. With such passion, she expected him to press for more, to feel his tongue slip past her lips, but he pulled back, releasing her and pressing a tender kiss against each cheek then resting his forehead against hers. She opened her eyes to see his were so golden they were almost glowing, both of their chests heaving.

Her alarm sounded, pulling her from the best dream she'd had in months. She pressed her fingertips against her lips and closed her eyes. She could still remember the way he tasted. The dream had been so vivid it left her feeling almost hungover, but she didn't have time to dwell on it. She had to get ready for school.

The second to last Friday of her high school career passed like every other Friday with finals before it. She wasn't sure why she expected it to be different. The only indication of how close they were to the end was a hint of excitement in the air. The topic of the animal attack was yesterday's news, and everyone seemed to be talking about the end-of-the-year parties. Even at lunch, Callie could tell Conall didn't really want to discuss the attacks, his frustration over their lack of progress radiating off him.

"Call me when you get done with work?" Ianthe asked as they walked to their cars.

"Yes, Mom," she replied.

"I'm serious." Ianthe smacked her arm playfully. "Don't make me worry about you." She narrowed her eyes into her best intimidating stare.

"I promise. I'll text you when I get to my car. Now, go deal with that brooding man of yours. He was kind of killing the mood at lunch."

Ianthe sighed. "I know. He's not used to something evading him like that. He just wants to find whatever it is before it hurts anyone else. Be careful."

"I will. Love you!" She gave her a quick squeeze before trotting off to her own car.

Her first training session had done nothing to prepare her for the Friday night frenzy. They were slammed her entire shift. She was tossed into the deep end, but thankfully she was a fast learner and already knew how to swim. Steve didn't seem as bad as the other day, hopefully because she somehow managed to impress him with her adaptability and the fact that she didn't mess anything up. She was grateful for Vicki's constant banter and humor keeping her smiling. She met George and made sure to keep her phone out of sight, not that she had a spare moment to check it anyway.

She was in the middle of mopping the floor and Vicki was wiping down the machines when Steve came out from the kitchen, finished with putting away the toppings. "I'm heading out. George is in the back, so let him know when you're done cleaning up. Lock up behind me?"

Callie mock saluted him and followed him to the door.

"You did good today." He nodded once and strode out.

Vicki whistled. "Wow, a compliment on your second day—you must have made quite the impression."

"I know, right? I guess there's no stopping how awesome I am." Her cheeky grin grew as Vicki pulled out her phone and put some music on for them to listen to while they cleaned. Mopping didn't seem so bad when she had someone else belting Sia lyrics along with her.

Vicki flung her rag into the sink, and Callie glanced at her phone as she finished stowing the mop away. It was a little past eleven o'clock. "Ugh, I'm ready to blow this popsicle stand. What about you?" Vicki asked as they grabbed their purses.

"Let's do this." With her belongings in hand, she knocked on the doorframe of George's office. He startled as if he had forgotten they were still there, which was interesting seeing as they had been blasting music for the past 45 minutes.

"Everything's all clean, so we're going to head out now."

"Uh, yeah, sure. Sounds good." He focused his gaze back on the computer screen.

"Do you need to lock up after us?"

"I will, don't worry." She was clearly dismissed.

How heroic of him to offer to walk us to our cars, she snorted. *Well, Vicki did say he was worse than Steve.* She had no doubt Steve would have had the decency to at least offer to walk them to their cars being that it was nearing midnight, not to mention the fact that something had been stalking their sleepy town.

She was lost in her own thoughts and scolded herself when she realized they had already reached the alley behind the shop. She needed to be more observant and pay better attention. Ianthe would chew her up and spit her out if she knew she was walking to her car at night without being vigilant, even if she was with someone. Vicki was telling her about some party she'd gone to the weekend before while smacking on some gum, but Callie hadn't heard a word.

A breeze blew through, causing chills to race down her spine. She scratched her head when she saw the number of cars left in the lot. There were three others beside hers, and she knew for a fact that their shop was the only one still open.

Vicki was telling her about some girl puking on some boy mid-make-out when she realized Callie was no longer with her. She studied Callie's concerned expression. "What's up?"

Callie's brow furrowed, noting the black Toyota Corolla with one of those *My child is an honor student* bumper stickers. "What kind of car does Steve drive?"

Vicki popped a bubble in her gum. "His mom's Corolla. Why?"

The hair on the back of Callie's neck stood up. "Is it black?"

Vicki nodded, her eyes widening as Callie's narrowed on the vehicle behind her. She spun around and swallowed her gum.

"Do you think maybe he got a ride with a friend or went somewhere else?" Callie asked, hoping for the best but at the same time already knowing what the answer would be.

"No, all he kept talking about was cramming for finals this weekend." Callie took a few steps toward the car, but Vicki froze in place. "Should we get George?" Her voice squeaked behind Callie.

She briefly considered that option but knew George would probably blow them off as overreacting and not even investigate. The cold sinking feeling in her gut was telling her something was very, very wrong, and she didn't want anyone to not take this seriously. She approached the car cautiously and paused to see if she heard anything, but the only sounds were her own pounding pulse and Vicki's rapid breathing behind her.

"Vicki, do you have Steve's number in your phone?" When Callie didn't hear a reply, she turned back to see Vicki nodding. She was now close enough to see in the car windows. No one was inside. "Can you call it?" Vicki tapped on her phone and then held it up to her ear.

They both jumped when they heard a ringtone coming from the bushes past the car. "Shit." Callie exhaled and looked down at the ground, scanning for the phone, and she noticed the dark puddle her right shoe was now resting in. "Vicki, hang up and dial 911. NOW!" She stepped back and tried to hold down the bile rising in her throat. She swallowed hard and stepped around the puddle toward the bushes.

Vicki put the phone on speaker, and Callie heard the operator answer. "911. What's your emergency?"

"Um—my friend and I were walking to our cars—and we think—we—know something happened to our co-worker," Vicki explained through shaky breaths and barely suppressed sobs.

Callie stopped short when she saw a shoe in front of the bushes. It was the same red and white tennis shoe that had been on Steve's foot earlier that evening, only now there was more red than white. She could hear Vicki giving the address to the operator as she stepped closer, a stone of dread resting in her belly.

"S-Steve?" she asked hesitantly, even though she already knew he likely wouldn't answer. She peered over the small copse of shrubs, and what she saw would haunt her for the rest of her life. It was more horrific than she could imagine, like a scene from *The Walking Dead* where a person has been ripped open by Walkers, insides on the outside, except this wasn't a TV show, wasn't some stranger. This was someone she knew, and there was blood, so much blood—*too* much blood. She stumbled backward a few steps, almost tripping then turning around before emptying the contents of her stomach.

"Callie?" Vicki's voice was small and hesitant.

"Don't come any closer. Seriously, Vicki, stay right where you are."

Vicki froze a foot from the car, the phone still clutched in her hand, the 911 operator's voice asking questions in the distance.

"Is help on the way?" Callie asked quietly.

Vicki nodded just as they heard something move, rustling leaves a few yards away.

"Is that Steve?" Vicki asked hopefully, but Callie was already sprinting away and not slowing down one bit. She didn't want to stick around and be the creature's next meal.

"Run!" she yelled, grabbing Vicki's free hand as she moved past her and pulling her along. They both ran for dear life back to Yogurt Land, thankful George hadn't locked the door yet. They threw it open and slammed it closed behind them, locking it just as their boss rounded the corner, bat in hand due to the commotion.

"What the hell—" he boomed as they heard the sirens in the distance. He put himself between the door and the girls after taking one look at them, bat still in hand. It was only then that Callie noticed the bloody footprints marring the previously clean floor. Her stomach churned again when she noticed the red around the white toe of her black Converse.

When a knock sounded on the door, Vicki squeaked and they all tensed visibly, but it was only the police. George put the bat down on the counter and took down two chairs for Callie and Vicki to sit in. Vicki sobbed as Callie told the police what she had seen, and even George looked like he was about to be sick as she described the scene. It was almost surreal. Your mind wants to protect you from something horrific, so it removes you, like you're watching it in third person. She watched as the police confiscated her bloody shoes as evidence, Vicki continued to sob, and she and George answered questions. She watched as Vicki's parents came to get her and she fell into her dad's arms. She nodded to George as he asked her who she wanted him to call, but she didn't want Grams or her mom anywhere near this. They would eventually hear about it, but if they knew she'd discovered the body, they would never let her come back to work, and she desperately needed the job. She tapped her phone's screen, pulling up Ianthe's number, and all it took was three little words before her best friend was on her way. "I need you."

CHAPTER 8

IT DIDN'T TAKE long for Ianthe to arrive with Conall by her side. Once he saw that Callie was okay, he wandered out of the shop, presumably toward the crime scene, seemingly fading into the darkness. Ianthe didn't hesitate to shove her way past the cops and gather Callie into her arms. She held her and rocked her back and forth while she sobbed and told her what had happened. She then insisted that Callie spend the night at her place, which Callie agreed to. Ianthe snuck away to call Grams for her.

"So, we're going to be closed this weekend until we can get this all sorted." George clapped a hand on her shoulder in what was meant to be a comforting gesture, but the way his hand trembled told her he was just as shaken as she and Vicki were. He sniffed once and gave her a squeeze before releasing his grip. "I'll call you and Vicki when I know more."

She was grateful when Ianthe insisted on driving and coming back for her car later. She couldn't handle the idea of going anywhere near that parking lot, not to mention the cops had blocked part of it off as a crime scene. Her stomach churned again as she closed her eyes only to see the image of his body flash against her eyelids, and she knew sleep would be hard to come by.

When they arrived back at Ianthe's house, Ianthe's dad, Joel, took one look at Callie and jumped up from where he was working at the kitchen table. She must have looked a mess with her red swollen eyes, pale skin, and bare feet. She heard Ianthe tell him what had happened and was surprised when his arms wrapped around her tightly. Joel wasn't usually an affectionate guy, but she knew he had been trying a lot harder to be a better dad, and she was touched he would care enough about her to comfort her. He released her and made the girls some hot cocoa, insisting it would help them sleep. He left the kitchen to call her Grams and explain everything. She drank the cocoa, and while it warmed the chill that had settled in her bones, she didn't taste much of it. Joel reentered the kitchen, telling her Grams was concerned but happy to know she was safe and staying with Ianthe. She nodded, realizing her cup was now empty, and placed it on the table. "Thanks." In a daze, she silently stumbled up the stairs after her friend and tried to ignore the concerned looks she received from both of them.

After the girls were dressed for bed, they heard a light tapping at the window. Ianthe opened it, and Conall swung over from the tree with practiced ease. "Any luck?" Ianthe asked, but Callie could already tell from the grim set of his lips that the answer would be no.

He shook his head. "I tracked it for as long as I could but lost it in the woods. Evin's still searching, of course, but he insisted I come back and check up on…" His voice trailed off, but Callie clearly heard her unspoken name attached. "Are you both okay? Is there anything I can do?"

His emerald green eyes shone with concern.

"Cal, do you want Conall to help?" her bestie asked her softly.

Callie's eyebrows scrunched down. "Help? What do you mean?" The implied part of the conversation was lost on her poor traumatized brain.

Ianthe sighed. "I'm going to take that as a yes. Hold your hands out."

Callie obeyed and Conall took her hands in his. Her brow was still crinkled when she felt a warmth emanating from him into her palms and fingertips, spreading throughout her entire body. She felt the weight of the night lifted off of her shoulders as a sense of calm and relaxation infused her body and mind like an instant muscle relaxer.

"Wow," she whispered when he released her hands. "That's a neat little trick."

He snorted in response, shaking his head. "Let me know if she needs a recharge." He gave Ianthe a quick kiss on the lips before climbing back out the window. "I'm glad you're okay, Callie," he called out before making his way back down the tree.

"So, what else can he do with those magical hands?" Callie waggled her eyebrows suggestively. Shaking her head, Ianthe smiled, glad to see some of her friend's sense of humor return.

Falling asleep came easier than she'd thought it would with Conall's magic running through her veins, but staying asleep was another issue altogether. Every time she would start to drift off, instead of the normal memories of her time with Evin resurfacing, she found herself in the parking lot approaching Steve's car, drawn toward it as if by some tractor beam, unable to stop her steps or look away.

After a while she even tried focusing on Evin's face and their shared memories (the happier ones, of course) to take her mind off the horror she had seen. She closed her eyes and took a deep breath, imagining her heart calling out his name with each beat.

This time was slightly different, but still the same parking lot, empty this time except for her car and Steve's. Turning her head this way and that, she realized Vicki was also gone from this version. She sighed, immediately missing the comfort her new friend brought to her. She hated being alone, especially at night in dark parking lots where she knew something lurked in the shadows. As if to prove her point, the quiet was broken by the crack of a twig or small branch from the woods.

She tried to tell her feet to turn the other way, to run back to the shop, but it was as if she had no control over them, and they took her closer to the car. "Steve?" she called out. "Vicki? Anyone?"

She stopped abruptly, noticing the pool of blood for what it was this time as it lapped against the side of her shoe. She swallowed, her mouth suddenly dry as her feet continued to round the car toward the bushes, but this time, instead of a red sneaker, she saw a booted foot.

Heart pounding, she jerked to a stop, knowing with utmost certainty that it wasn't Steve she was about to discover. Desperately, she looked around for anyone who might help her or stop her from continuing, but she was alone. "Please no, please no," she chanted, hoping her initial instinct was wrong, but as her feet pulled her to where she could see the body more clearly, she let loose a scream of anguish. His rich caramel skin was shredded and smeared with blood, but it was his lifeless golden eyes that brought her to her knees as she wailed.

Suddenly she felt warm arms wrap around her. "Shh-hh, I've got you. Close your eyes. Don't look," her bestie whispered in her ear, and she obeyed more out of her own grief than in response to the commands. She couldn't bear to see Evin lying there in Steve's place.

"Okay, you can open them now."

She did and found herself in her own bedroom sitting on her bed with Ianthe. "How?"

Ianthe smiled sadly and pointed to herself. "Mara, remember? I couldn't wake you, so I did the next best thing."

"Thank you." She hugged her best friend and took comfort in the embrace.

"Yeah, I don't think we've done this since..." She trailed off, not wanting to remind Callie of any more bad memories. "But I have a feeling we'll be spending a lot of time together like this the next few nights. If this is what helps you sleep, I'm happy to do it."

"Thanks, Thee. I have a feeling I'll need it."

"You know what I love best about dream visits?"

Callie shook her head. They didn't talk much about her bestie's Fae abilities, Ianthe preferring to ignore them until she'd had enough time to fully embrace what she was and all that it entailed.

"Upgrades." Ianthe smiled as she pointed to the new flat-screen TV on the wall. "What do you want to watch? Oh, wait—I've got it." A remote suddenly appeared in her hand and she clicked it on, the screen immediately showing the opening to one of Callie's favorite movies, Sixteen Candles.

"Mmmm Jake Ryan. Good choice."

"Popcorn?" Ianthe asked, passing her a large bucket of movie theater popcorn complete with butter on top that seemingly appeared out of nowhere. "It's completely calorie-free since we're in a dream."

"I think I'm going to enjoy these upgrades." She smiled and settled on the bed next to her bestie, the popcorn between them as she let herself get lost in the movie.

When she awoke the next morning feeling rested and grateful for the dream intervention, Ianthe was already out of bed. Callie smiled when she saw her backpack and a change of clothes on the floor. Someone had either gone to her car or already brought it back, but the clothes left her scratching her head. She sat up and swung her legs over the edge, intending to walk downstairs and discover who had gotten her things, but she blanched and drew in a sharp breath. A fleck of blood—*Steve's blood*—spotted her big toe.

The events of the night rushed back in, leaving her feeling nauseous and dirty. She scrambled toward the bathroom and yanked the shower on. Stripping off the pajamas she had borrowed from Ianthe, she stepped under the spray of water, turning it as hot as she could bear. Frantically, she grabbed a loofa and body wash and scrubbed at the bottom of her feet. She continued with her whole body and by the time she was done, her skin was pink from the force and scalding hot water, but she felt better, as if she'd been able to wash a little bit of the night before away as well. She took deep breaths as she roughly dried herself off. *You're okay. You're safe*, she repeated over and over again. She slipped on the clean clothes, brushed her hair and teeth, and wandered downstairs to see what the Grayson family was up to.

Joel was standing at the stove flipping pancakes while Ianthe stood next to him frying up a pan of bacon. "Hey Cal, how are you feeling?" Ianthe asked tentatively as she flipped a couple strips with her tongs.

"Better thanks to you." She tried to smile and show her gratitude.

"I hope you're hungry," Joel added, pointing to a stack of already finished pancakes.

"Are those chocolate chip?" Callie asked, noting the dark smudges.

"Someone told me they're your favorite." His kindness made her miss her own father. She wished he tried more, like Joel.

"Thank you. That's very sweet."

"Sit. We're just about done over here."

Callie sat at the table, which had already been set, and poured herself a glass of juice from the jug. Within a few minutes, Ianthe joined her, carrying a plate of bacon, and Joel brought over the pancakes. They made small talk while they ate, Joel asking the girls about the finals they had left and their plans for the summer. Of course, thinking about summer reminded her of work.

"I saw my backpack upstairs—did someone get my car?"

"Yep, Dad took me earlier this morning."

"Thanks. Was the—" She wasn't sure how to finish her question. *Was the body still there? Was the blood? Were the police?* So many possibilities, but she wasn't sure if she actually wanted them addressed aloud.

"They have most of the parking lot taped off now, I think because of the reporters that were gathered around.

Luckily, Dad knew one of the guys on the force and they let us through to get your car."

"He did say they wanted you to come by the station today for a couple more questions if you're up to it," Joel added.

Callie blinked at them uncertainly. She knew this wasn't a murder by anything human, so her answers wouldn't really help them, but maybe they would help Steve's family find a little peace. She nodded, swallowing her last bite of pancake, which had turned sour in her mouth.

"Since you're not quite eighteen, you'll need your mom or grandmother to go with you," Joel added, the corners of his mouth turned down and sympathy shining in his eyes.

"I should probably gather my things and get home so we can take care of that." She stood from the table, taking her dishes over to the sink to rinse off and stick in the dishwasher. She'd been over there so often and didn't like them to treat her as a guest. Ianthe cleaned up her dishes and followed behind.

"Thanks for the clothes. How did you get them?"

"Conall went over last night and talked to your grandma about what happened."

"About Steve?" She swallowed against the lump in her throat caused by saying his name.

Ianthe nodded.

If her mom and Grams already knew then they wouldn't need her to tell them about it, and she wanted to relive it as little as possible. "That's good. It'll make today a little easier."

Ianthe hugged her tightly. "I don't want you to go. You know you can come back here as much as you want. You're always welcome."

"I know. You guys have been great. I can't believe your dad made my favorite breakfast. Usually he just grabs us donuts or muffins from the bakery."

"He's been trying a lot more recently. I think knowing I'm leaving for college soon is making him regret all the time we lost." Ianthe smiled, but it didn't reach her eyes. "You sure you're okay to drive home? We can leave your car here and I can drive if you want."

"I'll be fine," Callie stated, but Ianthe stared at her as if she knew better.

Callie tried to reassure her. "It'll take some time, but I'll be fine. I'll let you know if I need anything."

"I'll keep you updated if Conall finds anything."

Callie retrieved her bag and searched the room again. "My clothes from last night?"

"Oh, they're in the wash. I'll get them to you later." Ianthe bit her lower lip.

"Okay." Callie picked up her stuff and trailed down the stairs. She didn't want to think about why they might be in the wash. In fact, she'd probably end up throwing the pants and socks away. The only thing she needed was her work shirt. Just thinking about Yogurt Land made her stomach roll, and she wasn't sure how she'd be able to go back there and not think about that night. She certainly wouldn't be able to park in that lot without picturing Steve's body. She shook the thought away. *Not crawling down that rabbit hole.*

"Call or text after you go to the police station."

"I will."

Ianthe hugged her one last time at the bottom of the stairs by the front door. "Stay safe."

"You too."

Callie sat in the car next to Grams as they drove up to the station. Her mom was asleep for the night shift at the bar, so she didn't want to bother her, and she was pretty sure her grandmother would suffice. Grams held her hand while she drove. She hadn't questioned her when she asked for the ride to police station, hadn't asked anything about the previous night, just offered her silent comfort, for which Callie was grateful.

The police questioning seemed pretty by the book. They asked her to give a detailed timeline of events, and she told them as much as she could remember, estimating on the time Steve left and repeating what he had told Vicki about going home to cram for finals. She explained how she knew something was wrong when his car was still in the parking lot so she walked over to see if he needed help. She described the pool of dark liquid on the asphalt by the driver's side door that she'd accidently stepped in, Steve's shoe, and discovering the body, how she had puked off to the side before they heard something in the trees beyond the lot and took off running back toward Yogurt Land. The whole time Grams kept a hand rubbing her back soothingly, only faltering when Callie described the body.

"What kind of monster would do that?" Callie asked, although she knew the cops wouldn't be able to answer her question.

"We believe it was some sort of animal attack. Did you happen to see what caused the sound in the trees before you ran away?" the detective asked.

"No. I felt the hair on the back of my neck stand up and

I could tell something was there, so my main priority was getting myself and Vicki somewhere safe."

"Okay. Thanks for your help, miss." The detective released them both and gave her his card in case she remembered anything else or had any further information.

When they got to the car, Grams folded her into her arms. While Callie had been doing well, holding it together while answering the questions, the warmth of her grandmother's embrace caused the tears to flow. "You poor, sweet girl. Let it all out. It's okay now," Grams soothed.

CHAPTER 9

THE REST OF the weekend passed rather un-eventfully. Ianthe kept her promise and visited Callie in her dreams to keep the nightmares at bay. Jordan had texted her a couple of times, but she didn't respond. He even called once, but she didn't feel like answering and pretending everything was okay when it wasn't. She was quiet and withdrawn for most of the weekend, still trying to process everything. Her family was worried about her, and even Sean tried to cheer her up. George called all the employees to tell them Steve's family was holding services on Monday, and Yogurt Land would be open on Tuesday. He emailed a new schedule out as well, having to adjust it now that he was down a manager.

Callie was dreading going back to school on Monday. She knew everyone would be talking about Steve's death, especially since he'd gone to school there. Ianthe offered to drive her that morning, but Callie needed her car to leave at lunch for the funeral. Even though she hadn't known him all that well, she felt like she owed it to him to go.

When the morning finally rolled around, she pulled herself out of bed, slipped on a long gray skirt and black blouse, and pulled her hair up into a bun. She didn't feel like changing at school. Her mother hugged her tightly and kissed her cheek. "I'm subbing at Sean's school today, but if you need me for any reason at all, call me. I'll have my phone on me, and Grams'll also be available if you need one of us to go with you today."

"I'll be okay. Vicki's going to meet me there. We'll be each other's support."

"I love you very much. Be safe."

Be safe had become the new motto for everyone in her town it seemed. It was usually said with such command that it was almost as if everyone were wishing the words into reality.

"I love you too. I will."

"Come on, Sean! If you're not out at the car in three minutes, I'm leaving you, and you'll have to take the bus!" her mom yelled down the hall before grabbing her purse and tote bag and heading out the door.

Callie grabbed a bagel from the kitchen, ruffling Sean's hair when he skidded to a stop next to her. "Are there any more left?"

"Yep. I saved you one." He smiled back at her adoringly, and she gave him a quick hug before handing him her bagel. "Here, take mine, it's faster. Mom's waiting and you don't want to make her late."

"Thanks, sis." Sean bounded out of the kitchen.

"Please Lord, don't let anything happen to my family," she whispered into the air, willing the words to be heard as she fixed herself another bagel.

"Bye Grams! I love you. Have a good day," she called

out as she opened the front door.

"Call me if you need *anything*, Callie-kins. Anything at all."

She smiled flatly at her grandmother. "I will." She closed the door behind her.

The halls were peppered with groups of students huddled together, talking in low voices. Even the normally rambunctious crowd was subdued. She saw several sophomores in tears consoling a sobbing girl, probably friends of Steve or kids who'd had classes with him. She sighed, shoving her books in her locker and grabbing what she needed for her first class.

"Hey, I tried to get a hold of you this weekend. Were you busy?" She glanced over to see Jordan leaning against the locker next to hers. For someone who was usually so cool, he seemed nervous, fiddling with the straps of his backpack.

"No," she replied, grabbing the last notebook she needed. "I…" She swallowed hard, unable to get past the lump in her throat.

"It's okay, you don't have to give me an excuse." Jordan's crestfallen expression pushed her pain away. She hadn't meant to hurt him. She closed the locker door, trying to figure out what she could say to correct his misconceptions while at the same time not really wanting to tell him the truth, not wanting to answer any questions about that night or Steve.

"I'm sorry. It's just…I wasn't in the mood to talk to anyone—"

"Really, you don't need to explain. It's cool."

"Hey Jordan!" Ianthe's voice sounded over her shoulder, entirely too pleased and cheerful for such a morning. Her voice softened with concern when she reached Callie and hugged her from behind. "How are you?"

Jordan studied the two of them curiously.

"Better." She sighed.

The bell rang once, warning students they had five minutes to get to class. "I better go. Jordan, I'm sorry I didn't talk to you this weekend. I swear, it has nothing to do with you. I don't know if I'll see you any other time today, so good luck on your presentation. I know you'll do great."

Jordan's forehead wrinkled. "Won't you be there?"

She smiled sadly at him. "No, I have somewhere else to be, but you'll do great." She walked away, pausing to glance behind her and noting when the information she had just dropped on him clicked into place.

"Shit," he hissed, turning his attention toward Ianthe. "She knew him, didn't she?"

"Yeah. They worked together, but it's more than that. She's the one who found him." Ianthe put her hand on Jordan's shoulder as he inhaled sharply. "Give her a little time, but don't give up on her. She needs all the friends she can get right now."

When she pulled up to the church for the memorial service, her chest tightened, her breathing shallow. She knew the signs too well and took a few moments to focus on steadying her breath after she parked her car. This was neither the time nor the place for a panic attack. She needed to hold it together. A knock sounded on her window, startling her, but it was only Vicki.

"Hey," she said, climbing out of the car.

"Hey," Vicki replied. They didn't need to ask how the other was doing or feeling. It was like they shared this strange bond, the kind that comes from experiencing something so horrific and tragic with someone. Callie grabbed Vicki's hand and gave it a squeeze. Vicki closed her eyes tightly against the tears that were already forming, swallowing hard and nodding once when she was ready. They went in and sat in a section toward the back where they spotted George and a couple other familiar faces from work.

The service was beautiful and heartbreaking. Steve's older sister gave the eulogy while his parents and younger brother sobbed in the front row. She recognized a few other faces in the crowd from school, mostly just people she saw in passing in the hallways. Vicki held her hand the entire time, both girls clinging to each other for comfort and support.

When the service was finished, George gave each girl a quick squeeze on the shoulder. "I understand if neither of you wants to come back, but please let me know so I can hire someone else."

"No." As much as Callie dreaded going back there, she knew it had to be done. "I still need that job."

Vicki nodded her head in agreement. "It's okay, George. We'll still be there."

George nodded once. "Okay. I put you both on the schedule for Friday night. I thought you could use some time at least."

"Thanks, George," Callie replied.

"And there'll be a new policy for closing that I'll go over with you during your shift."

"Okay."

George turned and walked over to Steve's family to offer his condolences.

"Do you want to—?" Callie asked, gesturing toward Steve's family. She sure didn't want to go over there, but she'd do it for Vicki.

"No. I don't think… There's nothing I could say," Vicki replied then tugged on Callie's hand, heading for the door. When they reached the parking lot, she gave Callie a hug. "I guess I'll see you on Friday."

"Seems that way. Call me if you need to talk or want to hang out or something."

"Does that 'or something' include getting drunk? Because I already did that, and trust me, it doesn't help." Vicki nervously played with her pink hair.

Callie smiled, glad to see a sliver of Vicki's personality resurfacing. "Probably more like binge some Netflix or babysit my little brother."

"You're on. I'll text you later."

She gave Vicki a quick wave before heading to her car, pausing after unlocking the door to glance back at the other people leaving the church. She noticed a familiar silhouette in the shadows of the trees off to the side. Her heart jumped and she blinked, and just like that he was gone, leaving her to wonder whether he had truly been there or was just a figment of her imagination.

CHAPTER 10

*E*VIN MOVED QUICKLY; he hadn't meant for her to see him. He should have been out trying to find the creature responsible, but each day without any clues drove him crazier than the one before. He was beyond frustrated with the situation. He should have been able to find it by now, unless…unless someone was cloaking it, hiding it with magic. He shook his head. *No, that's ridiculous. It's just some creature that accidently stumbled across the border. That's all.* He didn't want to consider the other option because it opened up a whole new set of complications.

He peeked around the corner to watch her climb into her car and pull out of the parking lot. His arms ached to hold her and offer her comfort. He hated that she had been the one to find the latest body. He knew it would scar her for some time, if not forever. He could clearly remember his first battle and seeing the bodies of his enemies, as well as his friend lying in the red-stained snow. He sighed, shaking the image from his head. It had been a while since he thought about that day. As a soldier, he'd grown accustomed to death, gore, and battle, but what haunted him more were the memories of the deaths of his mother and brother. Those, he feared, might one day be the only thing he remembered about them. *Focus*, he scolded himself.

He had already been to the crime scene, and they had found very little. He had been hoping for at least a footprint, something they could use to identify the creature they were dealing with, because while the humans would assume it was one of their wild animals, he and Conall knew better, but they also weren't positive which of the flesh-eating creatures it could be. *Maybe if I study the teeth marks*, he pondered, even though he had already studied the boy's body while it was in the morgue. The skin had been so eviscerated it was hard to pinpoint exactly what had done the shredding—tooth or claw. He sighed again. *We must catch it before it hurts anyone else.* A lump rose in his throat and he swallowed against it, refusing to let his fear for Callie's life rise. *I will find it. I will stop it*, he vowed.

CHAPTER 11

THE LAST WEEK of school dragged on for Callie, and not because she and the rest of the seniors were eagerly awaiting graduation. The morning announcements included reminders about the grief counselor who was available if anyone needed to talk, so even if she had wanted to pretend Steve's death hadn't happened, she was constantly reminded of it. It was hard to sleep even with Ianthe visiting her in her dreams. She dreaded closing her eyes and the images that would replay. The first time she tried to stay up and avoid sleep, she ended up falling asleep in the library the next day while studying for a final and dreamed of being chased, of finding bodies of those she loved ripped to shreds. This time it had been Sean's body, and she'd almost screamed when someone woke her up. Luckily it was Conall and Ianthe, so Conall quickly calmed her down with his magic touch. She could tell they were both worried about her, but Conall seemed mainly concerned that he and Evin hadn't yet found and destroyed the creature. It was cunning and careful, whatever it was.

There had been another attack on Wednesday, this time a young woman walking home from work, but the guys didn't seem to be any closer to figuring it out. Even so, Conall assured her that their list was narrowing, and now they had it down to two or three possible creatures.

While the hallways were filled with joyous shouts, laughter, and the slamming of locker doors, Callie couldn't muster up the same joy for the end of her last day of high school. Her thoughts were solely on going to work that night. It helped knowing Vicki would be there with her, but she could still feel her anxiety rising. Her phone lit up with an incoming text as she closed her locker for the final time.

Jordan: Smile. We're done!!!

The corners of her mouth turned up as she read his text. He'd been sweet all week, texting her at night with a different random question like would you rather have SpongeBob or Patrick for a best friend and why (Tuesday's question), or which is your least favorite flavor of ice cream (last night's question). He would always give her his answer after hearing hers and then ask her for a random question. It was nice getting to know him better and to have someone besides her bestie and her family go out of their way to distract her.

"There's that smile." She looked up to see him staring at her from across the hall. "Can you believe we're done?"

She shook her head. "It feels a little surreal, like at any moment someone is going to jump out of a classroom and yell 'Just kidding! You still have a month to go.'"

Jordan chuckled. "It does feel like that, doesn't it? What are you up to tonight?"

"I work till close." She swallowed hard, feeling her anxiety surge with the reminder of the last time she worked until closing. *Don't be a baby*, she silently scolded herself. Her mom had suggested she quit and find work elsewhere, but she needed the money and didn't really want to start a new job. She could defeat this; she'd put on the same brave front she had for her first day of school there when she knew absolutely no one.

"Oh right. Do you want a ride? I can take you and pick you up when you're done, provide some moral support."

"That's really sweet, but I'll be okay driving myself." She caught the slight fall of his face and felt guilty. "But I'm free tomorrow night," she added so he would know she wasn't turning him down completely.

He smiled. "No big graduation plans?"

"No. We're celebrating in the afternoon because my mom has to work tomorrow night. What about you?"

"Same with my family. My parents are having the whole family over for food and whatnot after the ceremony, but I was thinking about hitting up the big party at Olivia's house."

"Oh." Callie deflated a little, knowing that crowd was not one she usually hung out with. Sure, she had a class with Olivia, but they didn't really talk or anything.

"Do you think you might want to go with me?" Jordan bit his lower lip.

He's cute when he's nervous, she thought. She wanted to say yes, but if she rode with him she could be stuck at the party the whole time. "That sounds great, but do you think I can meet you there? I'm not sure how late I can stay out yet."

"Yeah, of course. I'll text you the address later." Jordan looked like he was going to say more but then a voice boomed down the hallway.

"Yo, Jordan!"

"Looks like you're being summoned." Callie smirked.

"Appears my wingman needs replacing," he joked, and she chuckled.

"I'll see you tomorrow at graduation."

"Yep, and I'll text you later tonight about the party."

"JORDAN, I know she's hot, but we gotta go!" the guy yelled, and Jordan blushed before Callie gave him a slight push in his friend's direction.

"Go. Lord knows what he'll say next." He smiled at her, and she felt a small butterfly flutter in her stomach.

"Bye, Callie."

It had been a while since a guy had given her butterflies. *The last one was—nope, not going there.* She checked one last time to make sure she had all of her things then walked to her car. She needed to stop by her house to change and grab a bite to eat before going to work.

Her interaction with Jordan that afternoon kept her mind off of things until she pulled into the parking lot behind work and reality smacked her in the face. Finding a space was a hard decision—did she park far away from where she'd found Steve's body even though it meant a farther walk, or did she park close to where they'd found him and try to block out the images battling inside her head? She sighed with relief when she spied Vicki's car and pulled up next to it. Walking through the parking lot and alley, she kept her eyes on her feet in front of her. The one time she wasn't vigilant, her curious gaze swung toward the spot she had last seen Steve's car, and a few tears tumbled down her cheeks when she saw the freshly painted cross strewn with flowers at the edge of the lot. When her eyes glimpsed a copper-colored stain on the asphalt, her stomach rolled until she quickly looked away, wiping her face. She hastened her steps until she was at the yogurt shop, where she took a few deep breaths to regain composure before stepping inside.

Vicki was behind the counter with some guy—Terrance, if she remembered correctly—and they were slammed. She quickly stashed her purse in the employee room and slung an apron over her head before heading out to help them.

The evening passed fairly quickly because they were so busy. Apparently everyone and their mother wanted to celebrate the last day of school or first day of summer, depending on how you looked at it. Terrance's shift ended in the middle of Callie's, so the last part was mainly her and Vicki. George was there and checked in on them frequently. He even got behind the counter himself when things got really busy, which was a rare sight.

When the last customer left and it was officially closing time, George locked the door. "Okay girls, new policy: if you close in the evening, the manager will escort you out to your car. This isn't some sexist thing—the same goes for any male employees. It's just safety. I would just…" He paused and swallowed. It seemed Steve's death had made quite an impact on him. "It would make me feel better, and I would appreciate it if you wouldn't fight me on this."

Vicki's eyebrows rose. "Has someone tried to fight you on this? Because I'm all for it. I think it's a great idea."

George's cheeks flushed. "Terrance wasn't a huge fan last night, tried to tell me he was a man and he could take care of himself." Callie flinched; she knew what was coming before he said it. "I reminded him that Steve was also a man, and he shut up pretty quickly after that."

Vicki hissed, and Callie quickly tried to steer the conversation to more pleasant things. "Got it boss." She mock saluted. "Do you think Vicki and I could play some music while we clean?"

He studied the two girls knowingly and nodded. "I'll be in the back finishing up some paperwork. Come get me when you're done, and I'll walk you out."

The girls cleaned in silence, and while they would occasionally catch each other singing along with whatever song came on, it didn't hold their normal playfulness. They were quick and efficient.

When they finished, Callie grabbed George from his office and he walked out with them, dangling his bat from one hand. Neither Vicki nor Callie bothered to ask him about it. They both knew he still had to walk back to the shop by himself, and to be honest, they felt a little better knowing he had some sort of weapon.

She turned her car over a couple times before the engine caught. She knew she should probably take it to a mechanic, but she didn't have the extra funds at the moment, so she just said a quick prayer that it would last a little longer and went on her way.

She could barely keep her eyes open, but she knew Ianthe wouldn't be getting ready for bed for a while. Her aunt Grace had just arrived for graduation the next day, so Callie was sure Ianthe had her hands full with family. She wondered if her own father would be at her graduation. He'd said he would and she had set aside a ticket for him, but it wouldn't have been the first time he didn't fulfill a promise. She could practically hear his excuses now: last-minute work emergency, car trouble, couldn't get a flight, missed his flight. She sighed. There were so many possibilities when the truth of that matter was she now ranked below his current girlfriend on his priority list. God help her if he decided to bring his girlfriend. She'd told him she only had enough tickets for immediate family, hoping he would take the hint, but she wouldn't have put it past him, and her mother definitely didn't need a front-row seat to that show.

Her eyes drifted closed.

"Couldn't we have taken a horse?" Callie whined as she walked behind Evin through the woods.

He sighed. "I already told you a horse would have been more noticeable. If you would just let me carry you, we could use my speed to get there faster."

She huffed, "And I already said you can keep your hands to yourself, mister."

"If I had known you were this difficult, I would have—"

She arched an eyebrow, daring him to finish his sentence. "You would have what? Not kidnapped me in the first place? Never wasted your time pretending to like me?"

He stopped, spinning to face her, his fists clenched at his sides. "I already told you I never pretended. I liked you, Callie—still do. That's what made everything so hard for me. I know you find it hard to believe me now, but I hope one day you'll be able to see that everything I told you was true. My feelings for you are true."

Callie crossed her arms. She didn't want to think about what his words might indicate. She had made up her mind that no matter what her heart wanted, she wouldn't give in to him again.

"Just take me home please," she finally said as she sighed.

"As you wish," he replied, approaching her and swinging her into his arms before she could blink, and then they were off. She gave in because fighting him was pointless if she could get home faster and never have to see him again. Then she could start getting over him faster. Besides, there wasn't any harm in enjoying the last few moments in his arms while it lasted, right?

Once they crossed the barrier—or portal, whatever you want to call it—he set her back on her feet and she swayed unsteadily. In the time it took her to regain her balance, the dream shifted from memory to nightmare. She looked down and saw her bare feet standing in a large puddle of blood. *"Evin!"* she screamed, but it was too late. A blur of fur flew from the woods and collided with Evin's chest, knocking him down to the ground. She couldn't make out distinct features, but the beast in her nightmare looked like an enormous werewolf with claws longer than the span of her hand from palm to fingertip. The beast tore and bit at Evin, eventually picking him up in his mouth and shaking him back and forth like a ragdoll.

She was just about to charge at the creature when the world around her swirled, colors bleeding together until they rearranged into recognizable objects, and she was sitting in her bedroom.

"Sorry I'm late," Ianthe said, sitting on her bed next

to her.

Callie's chest was heaving, and her hands were shaking.

Ianthe's eyes widened. "Oh shit. I'm so sorry, Cal. I tried to get here as soon as I could. I texted you and when you didn't respond, well, I hoped you were in the shower or something, maybe having a good dream for once, or even not dreaming at all."

Callie had no words, her pulse still pounding in her ears as she worked to slow her breaths.

"Come here." Ianthe opened her arms, and Callie fell into them, sobbing. "Tell Mama Thee all about it," she cooed, so Callie did, and only once she was reminded again and again that this was only a dream was she able to relax. After only a few moments, the girls fell into their new routine of passing the time watching shows and movies.

She woke to the sound of her alarm, reminding her that today she was graduating from high school. She checked her phone, noticing that Ianthe had indeed texted her, along with Jordan, who'd given her the time and address for the party. She sent him a reply saying she would meet him there and she was looking forward to it accompanied by a smiley face emoji.

CHAPTER 12

HUNGRILY HER EYES scanned the crowd of parents, landing on her family sitting next to her father. She smiled, glad to see he'd made it. As much as she didn't want to admit it, she knew it would have broken her heart and driven the wedge between them even further if he hadn't shown up. She hoped her mom was doing okay sitting with him. *And is that…? Yep, it sure is.* Her brother sat between her parents, with her mother right next to Grams followed by Joel and Ianthe's aunt Grace. Her smile widened as she stepped forward in line.

She walked across the stage when her name was called, her head held high, and she giggled when she heard Sean's loud whistle above the crowd. She shook her principal's hand and received her diploma. When she passed Ianthe's seat while making her way back to her own, her friend's hand reached out and squeezed hers. She stuck her tongue out playfully.

After their graduating class was announced and hats were tossed into the air, she ran over to her bestie and practically tackled her in a hug. "We did it!"

Conall smirked beside them, looking out of place in his cap and gown.

"Do they have anything like this in Fae?" Callie asked curiously.

"No. Children leave at different times depending on the craft they will study or apprentice in, or if they are joining the guard."

"Come on, let's go find our families. We can have more lessons in Fae culture from him later." Ianthe smirked. The girls walked hand in hand through the crowd, dodging in and out of groups of students and families.

"Did you see they were sitting next to each other?" Callie asked.

"Yep. I can only assume that was your Grams' doing."

"Probably. I wouldn't put it past her."

They were glad to see their two families were still huddled together when they finally made their way over to them. "Your mom would have been so proud of you, sweetheart." Joel's voice cracked, revealing the depth of emotion that one statement held as he gathered Ianthe into his arms, hugging her tightly before passing her off to Grace, who did the same.

"Look at you, my high school graduate," Callie's mom gushed, hugging her.

"How does it feel to be done with high school?" her father asked.

"I'm not sure yet. It almost feels like it's not real and I still need to go on Monday, or maybe we just got out for summer break."

"Well, it will feel real when we start packing you up

for college. I can't believe my little Callie-kins is all grown up," Grams said as she hugged her once her mom had released her.

"Oh, come on, Grams. I'm not that grown up. Besides, you have the whole summer before you get rid of me, and then you'll have me home for holidays and breaks. It won't be so bad."

Sean was next to tackle her, hugging her around the waist. He was growing up so fast, and she felt like once she did leave for college, the next time she came back, he might even be taller than her.

"Hey pipsqueak, no more growing allowed. I'm going to make sure Mom puts shrinking powder in your milk when I leave. I can't come home and have you taller than me." Sean giggled and released her. "So what's the plan?" Callie asked her mom, knowing they would probably want to do something before she had to go to work that night.

"Well, Joel invited all of us over to his house to celebrate you two girls together, unless you'd—"

She didn't even let her mom finish. "Nope! That's perfect!"

They all piled into their respective cars and headed over to Ianthe's house, where Aunt Grace had apparently worked the night before to prepare some awesome food, and her dad grilled burgers and steaks. Everyone seemed to get along well, or at least civilly, probably because her dad spent most of his time chatting up Joel and playing with Sean. When it was getting later into the evening, they bid their goodbyes and headed out.

"Text me later. I want to hear all about the party." Ianthe waggled her eyebrows.

"You guys could come too, you know."

"Nah, I've had enough parties to last a lifetime." Ianthe smiled sadly, and Callie hugged her, promising to text her later.

Her dad came up and slung his arm around her shoulder as they walked down the driveway. "So, you want to grab some dessert with me?"

"Can't, Dad. I have a party to go to."

"A party? But I have to leave in the morning. Can't you skip it?"

She smiled up at him. Typical for him to want her to rearrange everything around him. Their family didn't center around him anymore, though. "Sorry, I can't. I have a date."

"Marilyn, did you know about this?" he barked.

Callie was glad Ianthe had already closed the front door so her family wouldn't have to witness this mess.

"Yes, she asked me the other night, and since we didn't know if you would make it to graduation or not, I told her she could go."

"What?! Why would you think I wouldn't make it to her graduation? Are you kidding me right now?" His voice rose to a yell, causing Sean to whimper.

"Just let it go, Calvin. Don't start anything."

Her dad huffed. "Fine, but you will be coming to see me at some point this summer."

She took one look at his expression and decided to take the easy way out. "Sure, Dad. We'll make plans," she lied. She had no intention of visiting him over the summer. Sean would be going, but she needed to stay in town and work. They'd already had this same discussion—multiple times.

He gave her a hug and a kiss before he climbed into the

rental car parked down the street and took off, and Callie joined the rest of her family in her mom's car.

She parked along the busy street, assuming most of the vehicles were fellow partygoers, and sent a text to Jordan letting him know she had arrived. Olivia's house was in a nice neighborhood filled with upscale homes, the kind Sean called McMansions. She whistled softly, admiring the many second-story balconies as she approached the front door and saw Jordan sitting on the porch.

"You made it!" He gave her a quick hug, and she caught a whiff of his cologne. *Nice.* The butterfly from before flapped its wings inside her stomach.

"I did," she replied as he pulled her inside. The party was like every cliché teen movie you could think of. Someone dancing on a table—check. Teenage boys outside doing keg stands—check. Girls screaming as they got thrown into the pool—check. There was even someone puking in the bushes. Callie shook her head. It was hard to have a conversation with Jordan over the music as they wound their way through the crowd to grab a drink.

He handed her a red plastic cup. "Beer?"

She shook her head. "Just soda, if they have any."

He searched the countertops until he found a bottle of Coke. "You're in luck." Tossing some ice from the fridge into her cup, he poured her a glass, and she watched him the entire time. It wasn't that she didn't trust him, but her mom had always warned her about the dangers of leaving a drink unattended or letting someone else bring you a drink. Hearing about Ianthe's past experiences with parties also made her more cautious. Some mistakes were best learned through the experience of others. Jordan returned with two cups in hand, both full of soda, which she found endearing. They found a place to sit and talked or people watched for quite some time, discussing everything from classes to people at the party and what they were most looking forward to at college. Occasionally he was called away by his friends, but he usually waved them off or gave them just a few moments of his time before returning his attention to her. It was nice.

"Want another drink?" he asked, noting that her cup was empty.

"No thanks, but maybe we can take a walk outside?" The living room seemed to be heating up from all the kids dancing and stumbling around.

"Sure." He offered her his hand to help her stand and she took it, pleasantly surprised when he kept a firm grip instead of releasing it once she was standing. He tugged her along through the crowd to outside where some people were lounging around the pool and in the water—some fully clothed, others in their underwear. Plastic cups littered the yard.

"I'd hate to be the one to clean up this mess in the morning," Callie mumbled.

"Tell me about it. I bet she has a cleaning crew scheduled to come in tomorrow. Seems like she can afford it." He smiled.

They strolled around Olivia's large yard until they spotted an unoccupied gazebo. They walked over and sat on a bench. Jordan sat so close their thighs were pressed against each other. A second butterfly joined the first in her stomach.

"Thanks for coming tonight," he said.

"Thanks for inviting me." She licked her lips, a bit of nerves betraying her.

"I'm glad you'll be going to the same school as me. I've really enjoyed talking to you and hope we can hang out some more this summer."

"I'd like that too." She smiled as he leaned forward. They were seated so closely it didn't take much movement before his lips were on hers. She kissed him back, but while the butterflies were there with her nerves, she felt their kiss was missing something. She pulled back. There was no spark, no longing for more. She reached across to him this time, trying once more to see if there could be something between them, but she was sorely disappointed. Her heart just wasn't in it. This time when he pulled back, she glanced at her phone. It was a little past 12:30. "Crap, I gotta go. I have a one o'clock curfew," she lied.

"Okay. Can I walk you to your car?" He looked so hopeful, and she wasn't ready to crush him yet.

"Sure."

He held her hand as he walked her out and kissed her once more before she climbed into her car. She thought maybe the third time would be a charm, as they say, but there was nothing—no spark, not even a tiny flicker. She sighed as she started the vehicle after two false starts then pulled away.

CHAPTER 13

VIN KNEW HE shouldn't follow her. He should have been tracking the beast, but he couldn't help himself when she left the house alone that night. He only meant to see her safely inside, but when she came back out in that dress, he had to know where she was going, so he followed her.

He moved in and out of the shadows of the rather large yard where a bunch of human teenagers seemed to be having a good time. He picked up a forgotten cup with yellow liquid inside. It smelled like alcohol. He took a sip and immediately spat it out. "Ugh, what is this piss water?" he mumbled to himself just as a boy with a mop of black hair shouted, "More beer!" at the crowd while he chugged the yellow liquid, some of which dribbled out of the corners of his mouth and down onto his shirt.

Beer? I'll have to ask Conall if he's had any of this disgusting drink before. He licked the back of his hand to try to rid himself of the taste then he caught sight of her stepping outside with a boy. It was the same boy who had greeted her when she arrived. Evin knew he should leave. He shouldn't have been following her around like this. In the beginning he'd told himself it was only to make sure she was protected from the beast, but that claim had no weight now as she was clearly safe at a house with such a large crowd.

He studied the pair as the boy tugged her along, holding her hand. His fingers twitched, and he released a low growl. He wanted to rip the boy's hand away from her. Underneath his simmering rage, his heart ached. She was moving on without him, like she'd told him she would. He should have left. He needed to let her go.

He gave her one more quick glance, choosing the worst possible time to do so. The boy had his mouth pressed against hers and she wasn't pushing him away. In fact, he stared in horror as she pulled back only to be the one to kiss him again.

"That's what you get for letting a girl come before your duty," he scolded himself as he fled the scene. He couldn't bear to watch her anymore. Now that he knew she was over him, he needed to focus on finding the creature that plagued this town. He would find it and rip it apart with his own bare hands, because only then might he feel something other than the pain radiating in his chest.

CHAPTER 14

"FML," SHE CURSED with an exhalation as her car rolled to stop. "Stupid, piece-of-crap used car." She turned the ignition a few more times to no avail, not even getting a slight chug of life. She sighed, knowing she didn't have anything to fix this nor the knowledge to even try. She took a few moments to study her surroundings. At least she was familiar with the neighborhood. It would be a bit of a hike, but she could walk back to the party—although, remembering the state she'd left the partygoers in, she didn't think they would be any help, unless Jordan was still there.

She climbed back into the car and rested her forehead against the steering wheel. "Baby, I'm sorry for the things I said when I was angry. If you could just start, that would be great," she cooed, running her hands across the dashboard like she could reason with her vehicle. She turned the key one more time with only a click in reply. Realizing her car was indeed dead, she reached for her phone.

She exhaled sharply as she unlocked the screen only to

have the phone die. Reaching into her purse, she searched for her extra battery pack.

"Of course." She thumped her head back against the headrest a few times and closed her eyes, visualizing the exact location on the counter where the battery now sat charging, forgotten and left behind.

What's a girl to do? She could sit in the car and hope someone drove by at 12:52 in the morning, a highly unlikely occurrence in this sleepy town, or she could take her chances and walk back to the party to call Ianthe. She opened her eyes. She knew the risk she was taking by walking back alone, but she didn't think being a sitting duck in her car was a better option. She doubted locked car doors would stop whatever creature had escaped from Fae.

With her mind made up, she ventured out into the night, shoving her dead phone into her pocket. At least she'd worn a relatively comfortable outfit, a sundress with pockets and flat shoes, even if they were just flip-flops. She popped the trunk and searched for something that might help if she were to run across trouble. She had mace on her keys but wasn't sure how effective it would be against an otherworldly creature. Finally, her eyes landed on something long and metal. She removed the tire iron and tested its weight in her hand. She shut the trunk, figuring it was probably her best option.

Her flip-flops slapped against the concrete, and she desperately wished for rain to cool off the heat and humidity that clung to her skin. She had walked a block when she came upon the park. It was rather large and densely wooded with a clearing and playground in the center and several running paths throughout. Olivia's house was just on the other side, and it would have been a lot faster to walk through the park than go all the way around to Olivia's street. She paused, every horror movie she'd ever watched dealing with the woods and teenagers flashing through her mind.

"Nope. Taking the shortcut never ended well for them."

She tugged at the skirt of her dress, wishing she had changed before the party (she'd always been more of a t-shirt and jeans kind of girl), and continued on her way, her eyes scanning her surroundings vigilantly.

She was halfway to the corner when the streetlight she was walking under flickered. Glancing up, her steps faltered as the light flickered once more before cutting out completely. It was at that moment that she noticed the deafening silence. The usual chorus of crickets were eerily absent, and a chill ran down her spine despite the heat. She quickened her pace, her grip tightening around the tire iron she held at her side.

A strange, hair-raising shriek to her right broke the stillness. Her feet and pulse picked up their pace within a heartbeat. She didn't even risk a glance in the direction of the noise before making the split-second decision to veer into the park. Perhaps she could lose whatever it was in the wooded area. It had to be better than staying out on the open street.

She was sprinting through the park, careening through the trees when she heard heavy footfalls behind her. *Thump, thump, thump.* She ran for her life, but whatever was pursuing her seemed to be gaining on her. She turned for a second and saw its large shadowy shape before the snap of her flip-flop caught her attention. The front had caught on a tree root and she barely had time to register her shoe breaking before she was tumbling forward, arms pinwheeling, desperate to regain her balance, but it was too late. She lost her grasp on the tire iron in the process, her focus shifting toward breaking her fall.

She screamed with all her might, hoping someone might hear her but at the same time knowing this very well could be the end. She closed her eyes, bracing for impact. *At least I'll die knowing Conall will take care of Ianthe and avenge my death. I wish I could've told Evin...*

She thudded against something hard, but it wasn't the ground. As if her thoughts had summoned him, arms wrapped around her, and she felt the familiar rush of Evin's ability. She didn't realize she was still screaming until his voice was in her ear, speaking softly. "Shhhh. I've got you. You're okay. You're safe now."

She took a deep breath, her heart still pounding in her chest, adrenaline pumping through her veins. His scent was so familiar and triggered such bittersweet memories. She relaxed within his hold, her body filled with relief that today would not be the day she died.

She opened her eyes to glance up at him but was struck dizzy by the blurring colors and scenery they passed by at inhuman speed. It seemed like only minutes he held her, but she couldn't be sure how long or far they had traveled. A strong wave of nausea overtook her just as they pulled to a stop, and she shoved him away, stumbling a few steps to a nearby tree before emptying the contents of her stomach. He gently held her hair back while she heaved.

When she finished, he left her side, searching for something. He appeared a moment later with a small green leaf held out toward her. "It'll help." He smiled softly.

Grudgingly, she grabbed the leaf and shoved it into her mouth, trusting his judgment, knowing he wouldn't physically harm her despite how much he had hurt her heart. As she chewed, her queasiness dissipated and a minty flavor spread, leaving her feeling as if she had just brushed her teeth. Adrenaline still pumping through her veins, she blamed her racing heart on her near-death experience, not the fact that her ex had just had his hands on her. She continued to chew, uncertain what to do with the pulp in her mouth.

"You can spit it out when you feel better," he suggested, his deep voice rumbling with a bit of amusement.

She glared at him to mask her embarrassment as she turned to the side and spat out the chewed-up leaf. It was only then that she got a good look at him, his jet-black hair set in that tousled, sexy way, his golden eyes sparkling against his caramel-colored skin. He looked better than she remembered, and a small part of her stupid, traitorous heart fluttered at the sight of him.

She took a deep breath and glanced around at the unfamiliar surroundings. "Wh...where are we?" she stuttered, fear icing her veins. She knew the answer before he opened his mouth, her heart now pounding for a completely different reason. "Please tell me you're not that much of an idiot!"

"It was the first safe place I could think of!" he retorted, crossing his arms like a petulant child.

"Really, Evin? *The Fae realm*? You thought Fae would be a safe place to take *me*?" She crossed her own arms in defiance, disbelief and sarcasm lacing her words. "Because that worked out *so* well last time."

He flinched slightly at the accusation in her voice and then shrugged sheepishly. "Well, when you put it like that..."

"I can't believe you!" she huffed. "Just take me home, please."

"What? No Thank you for saving my life, Evin?" he cooed in falsetto. *"Wow, what amazing timing you have,*

Evin. You're my hero, Evin."

She glared. "Fine, thank you for saving me from whatever *that* was, but can you take me home now?"

"Nope."

"No?"

"That's correct."

"Then take me to Conall and Ianthe."

"Can't do that either, sweetheart." He arched an eyebrow, silently challenging her.

"Fine. I'll find my own way back." She knew she was being a brat, but she couldn't help it. He set her teeth on edge, and after what she'd just gone through, the last thing she wanted to do was remain around him and battle her aching heart with logic.

She turned and started to stomp away as best she could on shaky legs. Her broken flip-flop slid off of her left foot, and she noticed the smear of blood on the sole. Whatever had broken her shoe earlier had apparently scraped her foot as well.

"Great, just great," she muttered, ignoring the pain and stepping cautiously over to her broken flip-flop. She shook her head at the detached thong piece that should have held it to her foot as she heard his chuckle.

"Come on, Callie, quit being stubborn."

She squeezed the flip-flop in her hand and continued to limp away from him with just one shoe.

He moved so quickly he practically materialized out of thin air in front of her. She jumped, startled by his sudden appearance. "Damnit, Evin! Don't use your Fae magic on me."

"I'm not using it on you."

"*Around* me—whatever, you know what I mean."

"Well, I didn't hear you complaining when I used my ability to save your life," he spat out.

She stopped and took a few deep breaths, getting her own emotions under control while wondering what he was thinking. Why did he save me? How did he get there so fast? Was he following me? Could he still...no. She shook her head, dispelling the thought that her bestie might have been right. She can't be. Never mind—it doesn't matter even if she is right. It will never work, just as I said. He probably would've saved anyone in my position.

"I'm sorry, you just startled me is all. I'd appreciate if you wouldn't do that again...like ever. Now, I need to get home or Thee will start to worry."

"I already told you I can't let you do that."

"I'm not asking you to *let* me do anything. I'm telling you I'm going home." She narrowed her eyes, attempting to step past him, but a rock underneath her already injured foot caused her to yelp and stagger.

He caught her in his arms and steadied her. "What's wrong?"

"Nothing, just stepped on a rock."

Evin bent down and picked up the rock she had just stepped on, a few drops of blood smeared on its surface.

His nostrils flared as he rubbed his thumb across the still wet red smear and his amber eyes took on an other-worldly glow. He lifted her left foot gently but firmly and drew in a sharp breath when he saw her wound. Interested in what had him so worried, she glanced down. There was a cut on the ball of her foot, but it wasn't gushing blood, only a slight trickle.

"It's nothing. I'm fine. Don't worry." She attempted to

shake his grip from her ankle.

"When did this happen?" All amusement was erased from his tone, replaced by an icy seriousness.

"I'm guessing back when I tripped into you at the park."

"Shit." He dropped her ankle like it burned him and stalked away, tugging a hand through his hair. She watched him pace back and forth a few times before facing her again. "Are you sure?" His wide eyes pleaded with hers, but she wasn't sure what he wanted her to say.

"Pretty sure, but it's really not a big deal."

Closing his eyes and shaking his head, he said, "Oh, how wrong you are, *mo rua.*" His voice was soft and gentle but didn't soothe her one bit.

Stuck on the word *wrong*, she missed whatever else he said. She sat down in the grass and pulled her foot toward her face to inspect the scrape. It didn't look like anything serious. "It doesn't look that bad, probably not even stitches-worthy. It may be a little tender right now, but it will heal up in no time."

He sighed again, this time squatting in front of her. He attempted to mask whatever he was feeling, but she could still see regret lingering in his eyes, along with a little fear. Was he afraid of how she was going to react to what he said next or of something else? Something worse? "Callie." He reached out and put a hand on her shoulder, and she let it rest there, forgetting her earlier irritation with him when she read the concern in his face. "I'm sorry, but you truly can't go home right now."

"Fine, then take me to Ianthe's place."

"I can't do that either."

"I don't understand."

"I know you don't." His thumb stroked her shoulder in a soothing motion that did little to diminish her unease. "The blood…" He cleared his throat before continuing. "If you scraped your foot at the park and left blood behind, the creature that was pursuing you will be able to track you. I was able to see what we're dealing with. Quanliers are fierce, vicious, and sometimes singularly focused on their prey to the point of obsession. With the scent of your blood, you have now become its primary target."

She opened her mouth to protest, to interject that Conall could protect her, but her words froze on her lips with his next sentence.

"Once the quanlier has a taste of your blood, it will stop at nothing to hunt you down and feast on your flesh."

CHAPTER 15

IF SOMEONE HAD told her a few weeks ago that she would be stuck with her ex back in Fae because she was being pursued by a flesh-eating creature, she probably would have asked them what kind of crack they were smoking. Now, she closed her eyes, feeling the weight of her situation resting on her chest, her breaths starting to come in short bursts. She could feel the panic flooding her veins. She had only experienced a mild panic attack when she found out they were moving and she would have to leave everything she had ever known behind. This was so much worse. She felt like she couldn't breathe, like the world around her was spinning wildly and she had no control.

"Callie." His voice sounded far away even though she knew in the back of her mind that he was still squatting right in front of her. His grip on her shoulder tightened. "Callie, you have to breathe."

Can't he see that I'm trying? It was like she couldn't get enough air into her lungs; she was drowning on dry land.

"Look at me."

When she tried to pull her gaze up, she felt dizzy. *This must be what Guppy, my goldfish, felt like when he jumped out of the bowl when I was six.* Luckily, she'd been in the same room and had managed to gently lift him in her little hands. She remembered the way his mouth had opened and closed, how heavily his little body had heaved, trying desperately to gulp in water that wasn't there.

Evin's hands gently cupped her cheeks, drawing her chin up and holding her gaze. She blinked and her eyes watered, desperate for a solid breath. He pulled one of her hands to his chest. "Breathe with me." She felt the rise and fall, the pounding of his heart, which seemed to race just as wildly as hers. "Breathe in." His chest rose, filling with air. "And out."

She stared at her hand moving with his deep breaths.

His hands went back to her face, and her gaze rose to meet his, his wide golden eyes now a dark amber color, imploring her to follow his lead. "*Mo rua*, please." His voice broke, thick with emotion. His desperation broke through her panic and chipped away a piece of her heart with it.

She stared into his eyes, drawing strength from him, focusing on the rise and fall of his chest and slowing down her breathing to match his. It was a struggle, but after a few moments she was able to return her breaths back to normal. She had barely managed to get it all under control when he was pulling her into his arms, holding her tightly, whispering words into her hair too softly for her to hear. Her body, spent and emotionally drained, fell into his embrace.

She had spent this last year acting tough, like nothing could ruffle her feathers—not moving to a new town, not jerks or mean girls, not the email from her dad's other woman, not being scared to start over again at college away from the comforts of her broken family, not even having the one guy she had started falling for turn out to be a liar. It all seemed to crash into her at that moment, leaving her exhausted and grateful that someone else was there to take care of her. While she soaked in his comfort, that annoying voice in the back of her mind protested the entire time, reminding her that he was the cause of some of her pain. When the voice became too loud to ignore, she pulled away, missing the warmth and comfort of his arms.

"Are you okay?" he asked, his voice slightly breathless.

She nodded.

"Does that happen a lot? Where you can't breathe?" His brow furrowed.

She shook her head. "Not like that."

"But it has happened before?"

She nodded again, her voice barely a whisper. "Just once." She lay down in soft grass, not wanting to reveal more than that, not wanting to share that particular memory with him.

Thankfully he didn't push, instead lying down next to her, his body within arm's reach of hers. They both stayed like that for a while, not saying a word, sorting through everything that had happened in their own minds.

"What happens now?" she finally asked, breaking the silence.

"Now, we find out how a quanlier managed to escape Fae and find its way into the human realm."

"Shouldn't we try to stop it before it can hurt anyone else?" She rolled onto her side, facing him so she could read his expression, which she noticed he sometimes kept unguarded around her.

His lips pressed together in a tight line. "That was my original intention, but we can't afford that now. Conall will have to take care of the beast."

"Why can't you—" she started, but his movement cut off her words.

His sat up and stared her down with a clenched jaw. "I can't very well take you with me to hunt it, nor can I leave you alone here now. With you gone, it may lessen the attacks. The quanlier could be focused on attempting to track you and not feed for a while."

She mirrored his motions and pulled herself up to a sitting a position. "I still don't see why you can't take me to Conall. He's a skilled warrior and tracker. He served as the king's first in command for crying out loud."

"I told you that's not an option. If I take you back, you will be in immediate peril." He stood and faced away from her, staring off into the distance.

She pulled her knees to her chest, trying to unravel the situation they found themselves in. After a few moments, she spoke again. "But I don't—"

He spun around, his fierce expression cutting her off. "Because you're not his to protect!" he roared.

She narrowed her eyes at the unreasonable Fae in front of her despite the way his jealousy warmed her heart. "I'm not yours either."

He sighed and walked away. She didn't bother getting up to follow him; he had made it quite clear that he wouldn't be leaving her alone. She flung herself back on the grass. Again, she reminded herself that it didn't matter if he felt some unjustified need to protect her; the two of them would never work. She couldn't bear the thought of him watching her grow old and die while he remained for centuries. She couldn't put him through that. She closed her eyes, desperately wishing to go back in time.

She wasn't aware she had fallen asleep until she felt him lifting her foot gently, as if trying not to wake her. She blinked up at the night sky and propped herself up on her elbows to look at him. He was squatting next to her, wrapping up some wet, mushy leaves against her cut with a strip of fabric ripped from the bottom of his shirt. He tied it at the top of her foot.

"Thanks," she whispered, her voice still full of sleep. His hands stilled, still holding her foot gently. "How long was I out?"

"An hour or so," he said vaguely. "I was able to quickly notify Conall of the situation. Ianthe said she would make excuses to your family for your absence—something about a trip, and her father would help."

She huffed. "It's not just my family, Evin. I have a job to think about. Money I desperately need for college. What about that?" She hated admitting she needed the money, but it was the truth. She swallowed hard, wondering just how long he planned on keeping her in Fae. Would she even make it back into time to start college in the fall? She pulled her foot from his grasp and sat up, tucking her legs against her chest.

Evin frowned at his empty hand before dropping it to his thigh. "Conall and Ianthe reassured me they would take care of everything. I'm not sure of their exact plan as my priority was returning to you as quickly as possible, but knowing Ianthe, she's already thought things through and is most likely executing them as we speak. They both can be rather persuasive when they need to be."

She knew he was referring to their powers, but wasn't sure how they would help in this situation. "How long do you think I'll have to stay here?" Her voice trembled as she took a few deep breaths to still her rising panic and wrapped her arms around her legs.

"I promise I will return you as soon as possible." His golden eyes pierced hers, and she could read the honesty and solemnity behind his vow.

She calmed herself knowing that he would stay true to his word and focused on what they could do now to speed up her return. "Did you tell Conall what it was that attacked me?" She asked, remembering they hadn't figured out it was a quanlier before the previous night.

Evin nodded. "It helps knowing what we're tracking, but I wish that knowledge had come at a cheaper price."

His eyes held hers for a moment, allowing her to see the regret and worry in them.

"Well, what's the plan?"

"First, we need to get some supplies, including a change of clothes for you, before we track down a lead I have—someone who may be able to give us some information about how the quanlier crossed over."

"What exactly is a quanlier?"

"It's a hybrid of sorts, a cross between a human, a wolf, and a jackal. I'd probably describe it as similar to what you humans perceive a werewolf to be, but without the ability to shift into a human form. It also possesses unnatural speed and a taste for human flesh."

"Kind of like you," she added, watching as his eyes

widened. "I mean the speed part, not the rest, of course."

"Of course," he replied dryly.

"So…less Jacob and more wendigo?" she asked, forgetting that he wouldn't understand her pop culture references. He scratched his head and she sighed. "In other words, no cuddly wolf, more ferocious beast?"

"Try pure ferocious beast, one that now has a taste for you."

She gulped, acknowledging in her mind that he was right to keep her there but too stubborn to say it aloud. "Do you know how to kill it?"

He nodded, placing her foot back on the ground and leaning back on his haunches. "I do, but that may not solve the problem."

"What do you mean?"

"Quanliers aren't native to any area near a portal. They're actually quite rare these days and generally prefer to stick to smaller animals as their prey. We also need to figure out how it got there. I have a theory, but I hope it's wrong." He wouldn't elaborate more than that, but the grim set of his features was enough to tell her something strange was going on, and they desperately needed to stop the beast before it could hurt anyone else.

"Let's get some supplies then?" she asked, eager to do something. "Where do we go for supplies?"

Evin's cheeks flushed. "There are some things I need from my house, and I'll figure out how to get you clothes."

Callie's mouth went dry. Going to town meant risking discovery by other Fae. She knew the risk involved in him taking her there, especially if the wrong person were to see them.

"I'll make sure we're not seen. If we leave now, we can still get there under the cover of darkness. It will also give you a safe place to rest."

She licked her lips and nodded, knowing that while she didn't like it, he was right. It was their best option. "Okay. Let's go."

She reluctantly let Evin carry her, knowing it would be faster, especially since she was injured. She closed her eyes to block out the nauseating speed at which they traveled, blinking them open when he slowed his pace. She took a few moments to take in the beauty of Fae. The moon and stars felt clearer and brighter like the most brilliant diamonds glittering in the sky. They stuck to the shadows mostly, Evin peeking around corners before turning and constantly remaining aware of their surroundings. She glimpsed the familiar cherry tree in the dark, although this time its green leaves bore cherries instead of pink blossoms.

He opened the familiar sky blue door to his cottage and closed it behind him, turning a rarely used lock before he gently set her down. "I think I have some salve we can put on your foot," he said as he walked toward the stairs. She stared around the living room and dining room, remembering the last time she was there, how she had been sitting and eating with Conall when Evin came home and how protective he was of her.

He returned a few moments later with a tin in hand to see her in the same spot. "Are you hungry or thirsty?"

"Some water would be nice." Being back in his home was surreal. She wasn't sure what to think about it, and while it stirred memories, they weren't necessarily bad ones.

He came back with a glass of water and motioned to a

worn brown leather couch in the living room. "Please, sit."

She hobbled over and sat down, sighing when she sank into its plush cushions. He handed her the water and she took a sip. Remembering how sweet and fresh it tasted, she almost moaned when it hit her tongue.

He lifted her foot onto the coffee table, where he undid the crude wrapping and pushed away the moist pulp of what appeared to be chewed leaves. *Gross.* He opened the tin and swiped a glob of yellow salve onto his finger before gently smearing it across her wound.

"Do you think it needs stitches?" she asked.

He smiled at her and shook his head, slightly amused. "Oh, you humans and your need for sewing things together. You forget where we are, what I am." He blew across the bottom of her foot, causing the salve to tingle warmly and goose bumps to cover her skin. "Not even worthy of a healer," he stated, sitting back on a matching leather chair across from her.

She set the now empty glass on the table and yawned.

"Come on, let's get you some rest." He picked her up and carried her upstairs, mumbling about not wanting her to disturb the salve while it worked. He stopped at the top of the landing, unsure of where to take her next. When he started down the hall toward the room she had stayed in the last time, she stiffened in his arms.

"I-I don't think I can sleep there," she said sheepishly. It reminded her too much of the last time she was there, of being locked inside.

His grip tightened around her. "I understand," he said, his words tinged with remorse. He opened another door to reveal a bedroom she hadn't seen before. It was simple and cozy with a king-sized bed framed with natural wood that twisted and turned like tree limbs dominating one wall and a dresser of the same wood on the other. The gray and blue quilt he set her down on looked handstitched, making her wonder if someone had made it for him. "You can stay in here. There's a bathroom there." He pointed to the open doorway on the left side of the room. She could tell by the swords mounted on the wall and the scent of him—a mix of cedar and honey—in the air that this was his room. "Try not to step on the ball of your foot if you can. The longer the salve sits undisturbed, the better it will work." He stepped back.

"This is your room, right?"

He nodded.

"Then where will you sleep?"

"I'll sleep in the other room," he replied, continuing when he saw the frown that marred her face. "It's fine. Don't worry. Get some sleep. We'll formulate a plan in the morning." He lingered for a few moments longer then left her alone.

She lay back against the quilt with a sigh. Her foot still tingled slightly from the salve, but not in an uncomfortable way. The strap of her dress dug into her shoulder uncomfortably and she sat up, looking around the room. Her gaze slid back toward the dresser she had seen earlier, and she scooted to the edge of the bed. Careful of her foot, she hobbled over on her heel. She quietly opened a drawer, happy to find what appeared to be his shirts. She pulled out a royal blue garment and held it against her. Thankfully, it was a tunic, so even though she was tall, it covered her well, falling to mid-thigh. The fabric was softer than any she had felt before, and she brought it to her nose, a smile spreading across her face when she realized it smelled like him. She took her dress and bra off, placed them on top of the dresser, and pulled his shirt over her head. *Mmmm, much better.* She sighed happily as she slid back into bed, this time under the covers. The night's events caught up with her quickly, and it wasn't long before sleep overtook her.

CHAPTER 16

EVIN CLOSED THE door behind him, resting against it as his mind raced. *If I hadn't been there...* He shook his head, dispelling the thought. He couldn't stomach the idea of finding her as the quanlier's latest victim, but his guilt continued to eat away at him. *I should have stayed at the party. I should have followed her home. I should have done a better job tracking the creature. I should...I should...* He could have gone all night with what he should have done, but it wasn't going to change anything. He stripped off his weapons and leather guards, setting everything on the vanity.

He rolled his eyes at his own stupidity. *I should have at least grabbed something to sleep in before I left her in my bedroom.* There had been a moment when she'd looked so helpless on his bed that he'd debated sleeping on the floor in the room with her, but he hadn't thought she would allow it. Lying down on the guest bed, he attempted to get as comfortable as he could.

He was just on the verge of dreaming when her scream

split the air. He jumped out of bed, instantly alert. Grabbing his dagger off the vanity, he threw the door open and sprinted down the hall. Her screams still rang out, each one piercing his heart as he threw the door open. She was in bed, obviously still dreaming. Sighing in relief, he set his dagger on the dresser and climbed onto the bed. "Callie, wake up." He leaned over and shook her gently. "Callie, baby, wake up."

She thrashed against him, still in the throes of a nightmare. "Sean!" she screamed. Her chest heaved, her breaths coming in short spurts. When she began to sob, his heart broke for her.

He shook her harder, desperate to ease her pain. "Callie, wake up!" She sat up suddenly, eyes wide but not really seeing, and practically crashed into him. He wrapped his arms around her as she continued to sob. "Shhh, I'm here. You're okay."

"Sean," she whimpered through her tears. "He was…"

"Shhh. Sean's fine. The quanlier is on your scent now. You are its main target."

"But that's just it—what if my scent leads it to my house?"

He rubbed her shoulders. "It doesn't work that way. It's the scent of your blood it's following. Quanliers track their victims well because they can smell the blood pumping through bodies. It's worse if you have an open wound, like a shark smelling your blood from miles away. That's why I can't let you go back to your world until we find a way to stop it. Conall will protect your family in the meantime. He'll make sure nothing happens to Sean. He knows how much your family means to you."

She nodded her head and sniffled as he cupped her cheeks and wiped her tears away with his thumbs.

"Better?" She nodded again, and he released her. "Okay, try to rest."

He climbed off the bed but froze in place when he heard her say, "Stay, please." Her voice was so small and fragile it broke all of his resolve. He'd do anything to take her pain away. He walked toward a chair in the corner of his room instead of the door.

"No, with me. Please?"

He closed his eyes, knowing she was merely seeking comfort and he was simply the only one there to provide it. He couldn't ignore the way she still possessed his heart, but he also knew she might change her mind in the morning when she could see things more clearly. Hesitantly, he walked back toward the bed. She pulled the covers back, and he swallowed hard when he saw that she was sleeping in his shirt. He slid into the bed, unable to refuse her, and lay down, leaving ample space between them, which she quickly crossed. She turned on her side and scooted toward him, only stopping once her head was resting on his chest.

After a few moments, he relaxed and curled his arm around her. She sighed contentedly before drifting back to sleep. Evin, on the other hand, lay awake for some time after memorizing the sound of her breath and the feel of her in his arms. He knew this might be the only chance he'd get to do so.

He woke the next morning with her leg thrown across his and his arms wrapped around her tightly. She snored softly at his side, and he smiled, thankful she hadn't had any more bad dreams and had been able to sleep. Untangling himself from her, he grinned when she groaned at the loss of him. He pressed a kiss to her forehead and dressed, heading downstairs. There was too much to do and no time to spare.

In the kitchen, he put a couple biscuits on a plate and an empty glass on the table. He scrawled a quick note and set it next to the plate, grabbing one more biscuit for himself to eat on the way.

The stroll into town he took hurriedly, but not as quickly as he could have. It was hard to eat and move at optimum speed simultaneously. He passed a few familiar faces, waving quick hellos but continuing at a pace that indicated he didn't have time to stop and chat.

When he opened the door at his first stop, the shop owner yelled out a greeting. "Ah, Evin! Have you slain the beast yet?"

"If I had, do you think I'd be here so soon?"

The shopkeeper chuckled, the motion rustling his copper-colored beard. "Make any progress at least?"

"I have. It's a quanlier."

He sucked in a breath and whistled lowly. "Quite a beast that is. Wonder what would have brought it to the human realm."

"That's something I'm wondering myself. Have you encountered one before?" Evin knew Finnean had been quite the sportsman before he settled in town and opened his shop.

"Indeed. Dangerous creatures they are. The last one left me with a bit of a souvenir." He untucked his green tunic and pulled it up on the left side to show three ragged scars spanning from his ribs to below his pants. "Luckily I gutted the bastard at the same time he gave me that."

Evin hissed, and Finnean continued. "Need to keep

your wits about you if it truly is a quanlier. 'Tis one thing to study them and quite another to encounter one in the flesh. I have some things here that may help, but if you want a weapon that will truly defeat it, you'll need to travel to the borderlands. There's an animal trader there who can point you in the right direction."

"Branan." Evin supplied the name, already knowing exactly who Finnean referred to. He'd been putting off talking to Branan since Reid's death. He knew he should have told him sooner, but he hadn't had the courage, didn't know how to even start. How do you knowingly inflict that kind of pain on someone by telling them such grave news when you know it will break their heart and possibly even destroy them?

"Aye. You know him already?"

"I do."

"He'll be your guy. He can point you in the right direction to get the information and supplies you need."

"Then I suppose I'll just need a few things from you, some food to get us there and..." Evin paused at Finnean's raised eyebrows. He was taking a risk by telling him about Callie, but it was either that or steal some clothes for her, and he knew Finnean's daughter was about her size. "I'll also need some women's clothes—a dress and boots, something that won't draw attention to us." Finnean's brow rose farther. "And I need to be discreet. She's about Gwyneth's size."

"You sure you want something of Gwyenth's? There's a nice shop just down the road—"

"Discreet," Evin interrupted.

Finnean nodded. "Aye, I have something that might work. I'll be back in a moment." He walked to the back room, which Evin knew housed the stairs that lead up to Finnean's home. He'd been over a few times, and Finnean's wife was an excellent cook.

Finnean returned a little later holding a sack, which he passed over to Evin. "You're in luck—seems Gwyenth had a few she's outgrown. I put the least used one in there, and Alyss added some things. She'd come down, but she's not feeling well."

"Everything okay?"

Finnean waved him off. "She'll be fine, just side effects. You know how it goes."

"Anything I should know about?" Evin instantly went on high alert. Alyss was a partial Seer who had visions from time to time. Although they were mostly vague and hard to decipher, they had prevented some pretty devastating accidents for a few Fae around town.

"She didn't say, although she did demand I invite you over to dinner soon. Said you're getting too skinny." He winked. "She'd also be over the moon if you brought your..." He cleared his throat, dropping his voice to a whisper. "Lady friend with you."

Evin smiled, shaking his head slightly. Alyss had always been the mothering type. "Thank you, Finnean, and please pass my thanks along to Alyss as well. I'll schedule dinner with your family once this job is done."

Finnean nodded. "Good. Be careful out there. And don't worry—your secret's safe with me."

"You're one of the few I would trust with it." He grasped Finnean's forearm in a traditional sign of respect, and they shook.

Supplies in hand, he cautiously made his way back to home, where Callie was waiting for him, hopefully still asleep. She would need her rest for the long journey ahead.

CHAPTER 17

ALLIE ROLLED ONTO her back and stretched, waking slowly. She noted she was in Evin's bed as a recap of her nightmares and the night's events ran through her mind. She shook her head to clear the thoughts and instead focused on where Evin might be. Before she climbed out of bed, she looked at her foot. "Wow, that's some good stuff." The wound was gone, only a raised pink line remaining where the skin had knit itself back together. She found the tin of salve and smeared a little dollop over the spot for good measure.

Slowly she made her way downstairs after peeking into a few rooms and noting the silence that filled the upper floor. The living room and kitchen also revealed no Evin, but she did discover two biscuits on a plate with a note. It appeared he'd gone out for supplies. She wondered how long ago he had left the note and what kind of supplies they would need.

She had just finished the last of the biscuits when the door opened and Evin stepped inside. He smiled when he saw her and she licked the crumbs from her lips, using her fingers to wipe the corners of her mouth.

"Good, you had breakfast. Once you get changed, we can go." From the bag in his hands, he pulled out a forest green lump of fabric and two low-heeled boots. "I got clothes for you."

She took them into her hands, noting that they were somewhat worn but not ratty. "Do I want to know where you got them?" She wanted to smack herself on the forehead for asking that aloud.

"From a friend." He smiled, and her hand itched to wipe his smile away. It was a stupid thing to ask. She didn't want to know anything about any other women. Even if she had managed to convince herself she didn't want him, it wasn't like she wanted to hear about his romantic interests.

"I hope it fits," she mumbled.

"It should. She's about your size, although not as..." He licked his lips. "Curvy."

She could tell by the look in his eyes that it was meant to be a compliment, so she took it as one and tipped her chin up, daring him to say more. When he didn't speak, she took the clothes and climbed the stairs toward his room to change. She slipped the dark green fabric over her head, and it looked rough but felt rather soft against her skin. He was right about her being curvier than whoever had owned the dress. Where it probably hung nice and flowy on some girls, it clung to her curves. Thankfully it wasn't too tight.

She blushed when she noticed two scraps of fabric that had fallen to the floor—undergarments that must have been hidden within the dress. She tugged off her own, grateful to have clean ones and that Fae still wore similar things. The black panties and matching bralette were probably the most comfortable she had ever worn, although the bralette was a little snug. She took a few minutes to wash her own undergarments in his sink, dry them as best she could with a towel, brush her teeth, and comb her hair using his things. It was nice to see this side of Fae—that they weren't these mystical creatures. They wore underwear and brushed their teeth and hair just like humans, even though their brushes were made from wood instead of plastic and the bristles were most likely some sort of animal hair. She still looked quite a mess and had to take some time to clean up the makeup that had smeared under her eyes overnight. Once she felt presentable, she grabbed the boots, once again grateful that whoever had provided the items had possessed enough foresight to slip clean socks inside them as well. The shoes were a little loose, but they would do, and she preferred to have them too loose rather than pinching her toes. She gathered her own clothes and walked downstairs.

Evin was throwing food into his pack when she arrived. "Can you add these as well?" she asked.

"Of course." He picked up the bag he'd held earlier and opened it with a smile. "There's more, apparently." He pulled out a worn brown leather vest and a few wrapped items that appeared to be food. "Alyss thinks of everything," he murmured to himself.

"Is Alyss the friend you got the clothes from?" Callie asked, hoping her tone came off as curious, but judging by the way he smirked, he saw right through her.

"No need to be jealous. She's the wife of my friend. It's her daughter's clothes you're wearing, although the vest"—his brow furrowed—"is something I haven't seen before."

"I'm not jealous," she retorted as she slipped on said vest and laced it up, although, by the way it hugged her form and laced up in the front, she'd have called it more of a bodice. Her whole outfit reminded her of the girls she'd seen at the local renaissance festival a few summers ago.

His smirk grew as he studied her in the new clothes. "Ready?" he asked, shoving the last few items they need into his pack and sliding his sword into the leather holster wrapped around his waist.

She nodded, noting that the sword wasn't the only weapon he had strapped to him. She didn't realize how dangerous their journey might be until she saw him armed. She pointed to his sword. "Got anything for me?"

"Let's hope you don't need one, and if there comes a time that you do, I am prepared, but I won't give you a weapon until I think you may need to use it."

She nodded, rather relieved she wouldn't be carrying anything sharp. *Knowing what a klutz I am, I'd probably end up stabbing myself.* Annoyed, she tucked her auburn hair behind her ears. He studied her face for a few moments before stepping forward and reaching toward her face. She froze, unsure of what he meant to do. His whole body leaned closer, and for a brief moment her stupid heart hoped he would kiss her, but he merely untucked her hair.

"Keep your ears covered. With the new clothes, you shouldn't draw much attention to us, but we don't want anyone to have a reason to come closer and see that you're not one of us."

She didn't know whether his statement was meant to be a compliment or an insult. He studied her from head to toe once more, and his eyes narrowed on her wrist. He slid off the ponytail holder she always kept there. She opened her mouth to protest, but he spoke again.

"I'll keep it safe and let you know when you can use it."

"Fine. Let's do this. The sooner we get going, the sooner I can get home."

He draped his leather sack diagonally across her back and moved his hands to secure the buckle across her chest, but she batted them away. "I can take over from here, buddy." He smiled as she secured the bag into place and they set off.

They strolled out of town at a leisurely pace, only spotted by a few Fae who either ignored them completely or waved a quick hello to Evin as they passed. It was nice to see his world in daylight, not under the cover of darkness or at his insane speed, which made everything a blur of colors. She took the opportunity to study the houses and Fae they passed. Ianthe was right—it was like stepping back in time. The buildings varied between stone and wood, mostly with moss thatched roofs. The few Fae she saw were all beautiful, and their hair and eye colors varied across the rainbow. Their skin also varied in color, each tone having a sort of shimmer like gold dust or a soft, muted sparkle of glitter. She almost gasped when one smiled at them as they passed on the road, revealing his sharp, pointed teeth. Their ears were also pointed. She glanced back at Evin, but he looked the same as he always had. When they were finally alone on the road, she spoke softly. "Why don't you look like the other Fae?"

"What do you mean?"

"You don't sparkle or glimmer, and your features aren't as sharp. Your ears are like mine, and so are your teeth."

His jaw clenched. "They're not wearing their glamour. There's no point in wearing it in Fae when we're surrounded by others of our kind or humans who are either used to us or too entranced to know the difference."

"So, why are you still wearing yours?"

He swallowed hard, and his answer came softly, reluctantly. "I didn't want to scare you." His pace quickened, leaving little room for her to continue the conversation now that he was a yard or so ahead. She stopped, and even though his back was to her, he stopped as well, sensing she was no longer following him. *Does he not know me at all? He doesn't scare me.* Of course there had been a time when he had, but now she knew him, and she could clearly see that, while he had made mistakes where she was concerned, he would never hurt her, not intentionally.

He turned. "We really should—"

"Do other Fae see your glamour?" She crossed her arms, refusing to let the matter drop.

"No, it only works on humans."

"Show me." The need to see him in his true form burned through her.

He sighed, but she stayed put, forcing him to walk back to her. "Show me, or I won't go."

"You do know I could easily pick you up and carry you, and you would have no say in it, right?"

"I do, but you're not going to because you know it would piss me off."

He observed the firm set of her jaw and her crossed arms. He sighed again, realizing he would either have to deal with a supremely pissed off Callie or show her the truth. "Can we at least move off the road for this?"

"Fine."

He walked off the dirt path they had been following and into the woods a little ways with her trailing behind. Once they were hidden, he stopped and faced her. "Are you sure about this?" He licked his lips, a slight tremor in his voice.

"I won't be scared. I can handle it."

"How's your foot?"

"It's fine, and you're not getting away with changing the subject, pal. I want to see what hideous features you have that you think will make me cower or run away in fear." She meant to make light of the situation but immediately regretted the words when she saw him wince. He was scared of what she would think of him.

He exhaled roughly. "Okay, here goes." He closed his eyes, and it was like the magic cover melted off of him. His golden brown skin shimmered, and his black hair appeared even more silky and soft. The tops of his ears sharpened to points, and his cheekbones became more defined. She hadn't thought it was possible for him to be even more beautiful, but she had been wrong. He was breathtaking.

"See? No cowering, no running. Just you and me."

He smiled, and she had to admit she could do without the sharp teeth. Those were definitely a little intimidating. He must have seen her eyes widen because his smile immediately fell. "I told you," he pouted, turning his head away from her.

"What do you mean you told me? I'm still not running and cowering no matter how bizarre those teeth are to me. It's still you." She stepped toward him and put her hands on his face, turning it back toward hers. She gasped softly when their gazes met, his a mesmerizing shade of golden butterscotch. After a moment, she gathered her wits. "Thank you for showing me all of you."

He smirked and wagged his eyebrows suggestively. "Well, that's not all of me."

She shook her head, her thumbs sliding across his cheeks. Leave it to him to make a joke when she knew he felt vulnerable. It would have been easy to push him off and smack his shoulder for being a pervert, but she knew that was what he wanted, and she wouldn't give it to him. Realizing what a big deal this was to Evin, she wanted him to see the honesty in her eyes. "Seriously, thank you."

He closed his eyes, savoring her words and the feel of her hands on him.

She stepped back and tugged at the sleeves of her dress awkwardly. "So, where are we headed and how long will it take to get there?" She motioned for him to lead the way back to the road so they could continue on their journey while he explained.

"To the lands that lie on the border between Seelie and Unseelie territory. They're kind of a safe haven of sorts for Fae who don't recognize either court. It's an odd mix of people, some Unseelie who left because they didn't like the new king's restrictions or affections toward humans when he first took over, Seelie who prefer to pursue the darker side of their magic and thus aren't welcome in Seelie lands, and Fae who've been raised outside of either court because their parents or parents' parents left before they were born and have chosen to remain there. We patrol them from time to time but try not to get involved unless absolutely necessary because it's a gray area politically."

"And what are we looking for once we get there?"

"Someone—a friend, I guess—who may have some information that can help us defeat the quanlier."

"How long will it take to get there, and why didn't we just take a horse?" she asked, glancing at a rider who had just passed them as they emerged from the woods.

"My horse is kept at the palace stables, and I didn't think it wise to let the king know I was back in Fae. He would want an update on the beast, and I'd rather not explain your presence as it will undoubtedly cause other questions to arise—questions about when Ianthe was here pretending to be you. Now, regarding how long it will take us to get there…well, that depends on you."

"On me?"

"Normally I travel by foot at a much faster speed, so it would only take me a day or so to reach the borderlands, but if we continue at this pace, it will take quite a bit of time."

"And time works differently here than it does in my world?" She remembered the last time she had been gone and how it had only felt like a day or two to her but had ended up being close to a week in the human realm before she returned.

He nodded. "It moves more slowly in comparison."

"So, if we want to destroy the quanlier before it can hurt anyone else, we should probably move as quickly as we can." She didn't want to let him carry her, but she also didn't want anyone else to die.

"Yes."

"Okay."

"Okay?" He wasn't sure if she was agreeing to letting him carry her or simply agreeing with the idea that they should travel as fast as they could.

"We can travel your way, but I want to go piggyback style. I don't want you carrying me like some sort of invalid."

"You'd still look like an—"

She jabbed an accusatory finger in his direction. "I wouldn't finish that statement if I were you."

The corners of his lips turned up. "As the lady wishes."

He bowed with a grand flourish.

Callie rolled her eyes and, while he was bent over, took the opportunity to walk around him and climb on his back, wrapping her arms around his neck. He straightened and hooked his arms under her knees to lock her in place. "If you get motion sick, you may want to close your eyes." She felt the hilt of his sword dig into her thigh, but not enough to make her say something.

She already knew the swirling colors of the rapidly passing scenery would disorient her, so she closed her eyes. Resting her head on his shoulder, she couldn't help but inhale his sweet honey cedar scent. *Stay strong. Remember he lied to you.* The reminder of his betrayal didn't seem to sting as badly the more time she spent with him. She lost herself in memories and debates about forgiveness as they traveled. He didn't offer her much conversation, and she wasn't sure if he would be winded by moving this quickly. When her arms and legs ached from holding on, she squeezed her thighs around his waist.

He slowed to a stop. "Did you just squeeze me like a horse?"

"Well, it got you stop, didn't it?"

"So would a simple, 'Hey Evin, can we stop, please?'" He pitched his voice high into a falsetto to mock her.

Her cheeks flushed as she slid down. *Why didn't I think of that?* She felt like an idiot, unsure why her first reaction was to squeeze him instead of saying something. Perhaps it was all the horseback riding she used to do on their old ranch in Arizona. Her knees almost buckled when she touched the ground. He was quick to turn around and catch her by her elbows. "I'm fine. They're just stiff," she told him, taking a few tentative steps to stretch out her muscles and ease the ache in her limbs. They loosened after a few paces, although her thighs were still sore like she had been riding a horse. She opened her mouth to say something about it, but she didn't think he would take too kindly to being compared to a load-bearing animal.

"There's a pouch of water in the bag if you're thirsty, and there are also some snacks."

She was thirsty, but now that she was walking, she had a more pressing need. "Um, I think I need to…" *God, this is embarrassing.* She motioned toward the woods to her left.

His cheeks flushed. "Um, okay. Here, take this with you." He held a dagger out toward her. "I don't think you'll need it as we're in a relatively safe area, but it's better to be prepared."

"Thanks." She took the blade from his hand. It felt foreign in hers, but he was right—it was best to be prepared. She slid the dagger into a leather loop on her bodice that seemed to be there for that purpose and strode into the woods to the left, dodging bushes and brambles, hoping to find a good place to relieve herself. Luckily, she had been camping with her dad many times when she was younger and knew what to do. She found a tree and squatted, glad she was wearing a dress. When she finished, she gave herself a good shake and settled her clothes back into place. *Man, some toilet paper would be nice right about now.*

She wandered back to the road just as Evin appeared out of woods on the opposite side. He sheepishly smiled at her as she unbuckled the bag, set it on the ground, and searched for the water he'd mentioned. She pulled out an animal hide pouch and unscrewed the cap, sipping the cool, refreshing liquid. It tasted delicious. *If I could bottle this back in my world, I'd be rich.* She handed the pouch to Evin and he took a few sips as well.

"Take as much as you like," he told her. "We're not too far from the stream where we will camp for the night. We can refill it there."

Her fingers brushed against his as she took the pouch back and brought her lips to the same spot his had just been. She closed her eyes, taking the water in and remembering the last time she felt his lips on hers, how addictive kissing him was. She wondered if that was a Fae trait but wasn't about to ask him. "Can I walk for a bit? I need to stretch out my legs more."

"Of course. Do you need a snack? It's well past noon, and we haven't stopped to eat."

"Sure."

He reached for the bag and pulled out two carefully wrapped pastries of some sort, handing one to her before biting into the other. She sniffed it, curious as to what it was, then took a tentative bite. The pastry exploded with flavor in her mouth. It was filled with some sort of meat and the most mouth-watering cheese she had ever tasted. She may have moaned aloud—it tasted that good. Evin picked up the pack and slung it over his shoulder so they could continue walking while they ate. They moved in silence until she had finished the last bite and licked her fingers.

"Good?"

"That was delicious. Thank you."

"Alyss is a fantastic cook. I'll make sure to pass along the compliment the next time I'm over at Finnean's for dinner."

"Did you tell them about me?" If he was going to tell them what she'd said, they'd have to know she was with him.

He grimaced. "Not exactly." She arched her brow.

"There wasn't enough time this morning to explain our situation."

"Oh." She shifted uncomfortably and quickened her pace, angry with herself for being disappointed by his response. "I forgot to ask if you got in trouble with your king for what happened with Ianthe and me." She wasn't sure what had made her think about it; perhaps the way they'd snuck around the village and now knowing he hadn't told his friend about her.

He was drinking from the water pouch and almost choked. He coughed a few times, his eyes watering before he could speak. "It's kind of why I'm on this assignment, actually. The king thought time in the human realm might help me appreciate what I have for me here."

"I thought he sent you because you were his best tracker."

He laughed. "Oh no. I'm a decent tracker at best, but I was serving time at the cabin when the animal attacks began. Your local newspapers usually provide an amusing read, but that article about the death of the local convenience store owner piqued my interest. So, I sent word back to Lachlan, and he ordered me to investigate. He probably figured I should be the one to take care of it since I was already there. Saved him the trouble of sending someone else for a rather menial task."

She gasped. "Saving human lives is menial?"

"In his eyes, in the grand scheme of things—yes. He's more worried about someone figuring out the creature isn't one you're used to and putting the secret of our existence into jeopardy. If word got out of what lies just on the other side of a portal, all hell would break loose in the human realm."

"Does that mean staying in the human realm is a punishment for your type?" She scoffed.

"For most Fae, yes. Think about it—we're cut off from our friends and family, most of the foods and drinks we love left behind. We have to hide what we are any time we go out, and we have to adjust to a whole new culture. For some, it's the ultimate punishment."

"Does it feel like a punishment to you?" she asked, genuinely curious how he felt about spending time in her world.

"Not really. I do miss some things, but I happen to enjoy my time there." He smiled at her as if she were the reason he enjoyed it, but before the attacks, no one had had a clue he was around. At least, no one had bothered to mention it to her. "Are your muscles sufficiently stretched?" he asked, glancing at the position of the sun in the sky. It had to be late afternoon and she was sure she was slowing him down, but her thighs and arms protested at the idea of climbing onto his back again.

"They are, but I don't think my limbs can take much more."

"Will you allow me to carry you then?"

She considered her options and concluded that unless she wanted to put her muscles through more pain, there really wasn't a better option. "I suppose." He handed the pouch back to her. As she clutched it against her chest, he reached over and retrieved his dagger from her bodice, his fingers caressing her waist for a brief moment before they were gone, taking the dagger with them. He slid it back into the sheath along his belt and swept her into his arms, cradling her gently.

She closed her eyes, savoring his warmth as he picked up speed. It was strange to be carried in such a manner and to be barely jostled. He moved with such grace and fluidity, as if running on air. She rested her cheek against his chest and dozed off.

CHAPTER 18

EVIN GLANCED DOWN at Callie's sleeping form cradled in his arms. Holding her like that, feeling her in his arms again was bittersweet. He knew the complications that came with them getting involved if she ever forgave him. He wasn't stupid enough to think merely saving her from the quanlier would be enough to make up for the lies he'd told her and the mistakes he had made, but he hoped it would help.

He had been worried earlier when she'd asked about his punishment. How would she react if she knew exactly how long he had been checking in on her, how often he had been tempted to approach her but knew he shouldn't? He had accepted the inevitability of her moving on and finding someone who could make her happy, someone she could grow old with—someone who could grow old with her as well. He knew that was why most Fae tended to shy away from relationships with humans. Most dallied with them from time to time, but they never fell in love. His heart stumbled over the word. *Love—is that what this is?*

He remembered back to when he first met her and how she had captivated him. He would have spoken to her that day at the café even if she hadn't been his intended target. He remembered the first time he'd kissed her. He'd been trying so hard that night to flirt but also keep his distance, an incredibly hard thing to manage, but when she leaned into him and he stared into her eyes, he was a goner. It was just her and him, and she pulled at his heart. She was the only thing that made him forget all of his grief and pain, made him forget for just a little while that he was living in a world without Reid.

She sighed in her sleep, and he memorized the sound. He didn't think she'd allow him to do this once his job was done and the quanlier was destroyed. His thoughts jumped from her to the creature. Earlier when he was thinking about how a quanlier had gotten into the human realm, he'd remembered something Reid had once told him. On their way back from a check on the goblin market, Evin was hungover. He was having difficulty keeping his wits about him and staying awake, so Reid started talking about some of the various Fae creatures he was studying in his spare time. Reid had always been interested in the different animals since he was a young boy. Evin was sure, had his father not trained them to be guards and basically implied that one day Reid would take his place as first in command to the king, Reid may have gone on to a profession dealing with animals, be it a caretaker, healer, or trader. He'd had their mother's affinity for nature, which Evin lacked. While Evin could easily beat Reid in a footrace, there were some benefits to having more of his mother's magic. Reid had possessed a balance of their parents' abilities, and the way he'd used them in tandem had made him a formidable opponent on the battlefield.

Evin blanched recalling how Reid had tried to protect

him the night he drunkenly started a fight with Casimir. One minute he was fighting Casimir and the next his opponent shifted, suddenly appearing behind him. Reid threw himself in front of Evin, sword at the ready, but Casimir had already flung a dagger from his left hand at the exact moment Reid appeared, and it buried itself into Reid's chest.

Evin stumbled for a moment, his grip on Callie faltering, which jostled her softly, but she didn't wake. He pulled away from the memory, not allowing himself to drown in it this time, and tried to recall exactly what Reid had said about the quanlier. The memory of his brother's words struck him like a bolt of lightning.

"Did you know there is an ancient bloodline of Fae who can control animals with magic, can make them do their bidding?"

"Let me guess, you paid a visit to a certain animal trader yesterday." Evin smirked, guessing exactly where his brother had spent the night.

Reid's blush was all he needed to see to know the answer. "You know I'm never one to kiss and tell, so back to the question at hand: did you know there are Fae who can control animals with their magic?"

"You mean like how the horse master communes with the horses to train them?"

"Hmm, now that I think about it, he may be from that bloodline, probably a very diluted branch, but he doesn't really control them, just communicates with them. Also, I'm not talking about docile, harmless creatures. I'm talking about controlling the untamable, the wild and bloodthirsty."

"You don't mean..."

"I do. I heard of a bloodline that, centuries ago, could control quanliers, adjules, and even dragons."

Evin whistled. "Dragons have been extinct for ages. That would be some powerful magic."

"Think about it—you could get away with murder if you had an animal commit it for you."

Evin stopped abruptly, his chest heaving as Reid's words echoed in his mind. "You could get away with murder if you had an animal commit it for you." Who would have the power and motive? And why send it to the human realm?

Callie stirred in his grasp and he resumed moving. They weren't too far from the stream now. There was a cave nearby he and Reid had stayed in on more than one occasion. Some of their old supplies might even be stashed inside if no one else had used it. He slowed when he approached the steep slope toward the stream and cave.

"Callie, wake up, sweetheart." She stirred, blinking her eyes open in response. "We're here." She yawned, and he carefully slid her back onto her feet.

"Where's here?"

"Where we're going to camp for the night. There's a cave down by the stream, but it's a little bit of a steep climb down and I wasn't sure I could make it still carrying you."

She dug the toe of her boot into the ground as her cheeks stained pink. "Okay. Lead the way."

He stepped cautiously, climbing down when necessary and offering her a hand until they arrived at the cave. Their fire pit was still there, assembled. He dug around and found a pan he didn't think they'd need and a few blankets they would definitely use. They were old and smelled like smoke mixed with the woods, but it didn't matter to either of them. He spread one out on the floor while Callie drank some water then he unsheathed the dagger and set it on the blanket. "I'm going to gather some firewood and refill the water. Stay here please. I'm leaving the dagger in case you need it."

"Thank you," she replied, handing him the water pouch and taking a moment to take in their surroundings. The cave had a wide open mouth, tall enough they didn't have to duck walking inside, and it narrowed toward the back. She wasn't sure how far back the cave went but knew he wouldn't have taken her there if he didn't trust it to be a safe location. The fire pit was lined with stones, and two large flat rocks had been hauled over to serve as seats. On the floor of the cave was a fine, silty dirty that felt cool to the touch. She inhaled the earthy, smoky scent. Noting the supplies and two seats, she guessed this was somewhere Evin and Reid had visited often. She wondered how long it had been since Evin had been there and let her mind wander as she waited for his return.

Once his tasks were complete and he had a strong fire going, he sat down next to her on the blanket and pulled two more pastry squares from his bag along with some jerky. They made small talk while they ate and drank. She told him about finishing high school and where she planned on going to college the following year. When it grew dark, he piled some more wood onto the fire and told her to rest. They would most likely be leaving before dawn. He lay down next to her, pleased when she didn't immediately object to his presence. It could have been because there were only two blankets and they were already using one underneath them, or perhaps she merely didn't mind his body heat next to her, but there was a part of him that hoped it was because she wanted him there. Once she fell asleep, he studied her features in the firelight, pulling her closer to him so he could be comforted by her warmth. Finally, he closed his own eyes and let sleep pull him under.

CHAPTER 19

ALLIE WOKE TO Evin shaking her shoulder gently and whispering her name. Sleepily, she took care of business while he packed up their things and refilled the water. When she returned, he handed her a piece of fruit that was shaped like a pear, but its skin was purple. Hesitantly she bit into it, and an explosion of juice filled her mouth. It was sweet and fruity but also had a hint of rosewater. She licked her lips after she chewed her bite, hoping to catch any residual mess, savoring the refreshing and unique taste.

Evin, caught staring at her, looked away when she met his eyes. She was happy to see he hadn't glamoured himself again. She was enjoying his angular features and getting used to the teeth. To be honest, they didn't bother her that much. On someone else, they would have probably looked terrifying, but this was Evin, and she liked the way he looked.

"I'm assuming the stories about eating Fae fruit aren't true. Otherwise I'm screwed like Persephone. Although if that pomegranate tasted this good, I don't really blame her."

Evin tilted his head to the left. "What stories?"

"Hmmm…there are a couple I've read since learning about you guys and Thee. One said a simple bite of Fae fruit will leave a human so addicted they won't be able to function without it and will continue to crave it until it drives them into madness. Another said eating or drinking anything in Fae would mean you could never leave Fae." She chuckled, finishing the last bite of the fruit. "Guess it's little too late to worry about that."

"Do you really think I would give you something to eat that would cause you to be stuck here forever or drive you into madness?" What had started as a simple joke on her part had struck him in a way she hadn't intended.

"No, I suppose not." She tried to backpedal. "It was just a joke. I didn't mean any offense."

His brow still furrowed, he thrust their pack into her hands before stalking out of the cave. She wasn't sure what to make of what had just happened and didn't want to say anything more for fear of digging the hole deeper. It was still dark outside, which made hiking a little difficult for her, but the moonlight helped, and it seemed Evin had night vision. He navigated the sharp slope like it was nothing, turning back to assist her when needed, and it helped her to watch him and step where he stepped.

When they reached the top, they continued to walk through the woods. "Why aren't we walking on the road?" she asked, hoping to push through the awkward silence that had descended since her careless comment.

He put a finger to his lips, motioning for her to be quiet, and when he replied, his voice was just above a whisper. "We're in the borderlands now. It isn't safe for you to be on the road."

"Even with my ears hidden?" she whispered back.

He nodded in reply. "I don't want to take that risk."

They continued on in silence, him allowing her to walk on her own even though she knew she was slowing them down. When the sun finally rose over the horizon, she gave in and allowed him to carry her piggyback again. Thankfully, her muscles didn't protest as much after her rest. With his inhuman speed, they covered miles by the time the sun had passed overhead. Judging by its position in the sky, it was late afternoon when they finally stopped. Gently, he lowered her to her feet when they reached the top of a wooded hill. She could see a town in the distance.

"I need you to wait here."

"You want me to what?"

His lips pressed into a firm line, showing her he didn't like this option much either. "I know it's not ideal, but the goblin market is not somewhere you should be. It's too dangerous. I need you to hide here out of sight until I come back for you."

Her heart beat erratically, and she took a few shallow breaths, tamping down her panic. "How long will you be?"

"Hopefully not long, and the guy I'm going to see should have some important answers for us." He stepped closer to her.

"Answers?" She tried to ignore the rapid beating of her heart as he invaded her personal space.

"He's an animal expert of sorts. He should be able to give us more information about the quanlier, like how to destroy it, among other things," he replied vaguely.

"Okay, fine. Go," she pouted, jutting her bottom lip

out a little. "I'll just sit here and twiddle my thumbs while waiting for your return."

He reached out and trailed a finger across her mouth, his butterscotch eyes shimmering bright gold. "Be safe," he whispered, pressing something into her palm, and before she could protest, he pressed his lips to hers, stealing a quick kiss before walking away.

She stood by a tree, watching him go. He glanced back once to give her a quick reassuring wave before disappearing down the slope of the hill. She sighed and drew her attention to what he had given her, and she rubbed her fingers down the handle of the dagger. Since she had nothing else to do, she took some time to study its beautiful craftsmanship. The handle felt handmade, and the blade gleamed in the early morning light, appearing to be made out of an opalescent stone. The tip curved back, one edge slightly serrated. She bit her bottom lip, hoping she wouldn't need to use it against anyone or anything while he was gone. She slid the dagger into the loop on her vest then her fingers brushed a hidden pocket. *Huh.* She dug her fingers into it, pulling out a scrap of parchment. It was brown and crinkled, torn along the edges, and the words were written in a hurried scrawl.

Beware the lover scorned

What the hell? Why would someone carry a note like that in their pocket? Fae are so weird. Coming to the conclusion that it had probably been left by the vest's previous owner, she crumpled up the scrap and shoved it back in her pocket. She sat down on the grass and leaned against the tree, the exhaustion of recent events and their early morning departure catching up to her. She fought against her drooping eyes for quite some time—pinching her arms, stomping her feet, even doing jumping jacks—but she was just too tired. Finally, she pulled the dagger from where it rested against her and held it in her hand. *I'll just rest my eyes for a moment*, she thought before she drifted off, the dagger still clenched in her fingers, at the ready should she hear anything.

"Such a pretty thing should fetch us a good price," a voice hissed.

"So should the blade. Did you see the mark on the bottom of the handle? I wonder how she got it. Stole it, perhaps? No matter. Should fetch us a pretty price right along with her."

She yanked her eyes open, horrified to see two creatures crouched over her. They were short in stature and appeared bony, almost emaciated. One's skin was a forest green while the other's was a mossy brown color. Their sharp features glinted in the dying light of day, their ears were large in proportion to their heads, and their teeth were like tiny daggers in their mouths. She gasped and reached for the blade, but it was no longer in her hand, now in the grasp of the mossy brown aggressor. Her gut combined with all the fantasy movies she'd seen were enough to tell her these guys fit the goblin bill to a T.

"You idiot, you didn't tie her hands tight enough!" the mossy brown one screeched at the other.

She noticed the rope draped over her wrists and attempted to shake it free, but the green goblin was fast and tightened the binding. She swung at him and kicked, but her legs were also tied together. How had they managed to do that without waking her? It was then that she noticed her thrashing caused the ropes to tighten around her.

"That's right, pretty—those ropes will only tighten the more you fight them. They're enchanted. Don't need much more than a firm loop and you just let your prey do the rest of the work." The green goblin smiled at her menacingly, but his words stopped her fight. She tested his theory with one more kick and then gave in, lightly knocking her head back against the tree she sat against. Evin was going to kill her if these creatures didn't first.

"Throw her in the wagon with the rest."

The green goblin picked her up and threw her over his shoulder, which would have been rather comical if not for the dire circumstances. She could feel her toes dragging across the forest floor, and her head bobbed dangerously close to the dirt with how she was folded over his tiny frame. Her head throbbed with blood rushing to it, her heart beating wildly against her chest. She tried to take deep breaths, but his bony shoulder poked into her diaphragm painfully.

At last she was tossed into the back of a wooden cage on wheels. Her head hit the floor and scraped against the rough surface, causing a trickle of blood to run down her cheek. She curled into herself and lifted her head, raising her shoulder up to wipe the blood away, and that was when she noticed the others. Most of them looked like Fae peasants with dirty clothes, but a few appeared human. She wondered if they were humans, Fae using glamour, or perhaps even half Fae. As far as she knew, Ianthe didn't need to use glamour and she looked human. She pulled herself up into a sitting position and shook her head, studying the other occupants. There were eight in all, some bound, others not, but all of them looked haggard with a mixture of fear and defeat in their expression. Two of them appeared to be young children, and the one huddled in the corner wearing a dress blinked at Callie curiously. She had long, stringy, lavender hair, a blue tinge to her skin, and eyes that were too wide and too turquoise to be human. She reminded Callie of one of those dolls with overly large eyes.

The horse-drawn cart lurched forward and the little girl tipped over onto the floor, letting out a yelp. No one around her bothered to help her up. One man even pulled his legs up closer to his own body as to avoid any contact with the girl, and others stared out the bars or looked away. The other child moved to help her, but the woman next to him quickly yanked him back. Callie frowned. *What is wrong with them? Why aren't they helping her? Poor thing.* She scooted over to the girl and offered her bound hands. The girl hesitantly placed her hand in Callie's, and Callie awkwardly pulled her into a sitting position.

"Are you okay?"

The girl's hand felt warmer than expected, and she didn't pull it away, but she also didn't respond. Callie wondered if perhaps the girl spoke a different language and didn't understand her.

She motioned toward the girl's scraped knee and asked again, "Are you okay?"

The little girl cocked her head but remained silent.

"She won't talk. I already tried," the little boy piped up, and the woman turned him away.

"Don't talk to her, neither of them, especially not the *leathfuil*," the woman scolded. The boy and girl both flinched at the last word the woman spat. Callie didn't know what it meant, but she could tell it wasn't a compliment. The girl tugged her hand out of Callie's gentle hold.

"Oh, don't do that," Callie whispered, smiling at the girl. "I don't know what that woman said, but she seems like a meanie. Don't listen to her. It'll be okay." Callie said the words even though she didn't quite believe them herself. Her attention was pulled from the girl to her surroundings when she heard the voices of others around her. The goblins were pulling the cart into the town she had seen in the distance. The outskirts of it were filled with a bustling market. There were brightly colored canopies and vendors with a wide variety of things for sale. She glanced at the stalls they passed; one sold vibrant fruit like the piece she'd had for breakfast, and another held herbs in containers. As they moved deeper into the market, the stalls displayed items she didn't recognize. She blanched when they came across a tent with necklaces made of teeth and what clearly looked like human fingers.

"Where are we?" she whispered, hoping someone would answer her.

The mossy brown captor turned around and grinned at her wickedly. "Welcome to the goblin market."

She swallowed. *No wonder Evin asked me to stay in the woods*, she thought as they passed a stall with a collection of weapons made from bones and another advertising wigs made from human hair…with the scalp still attached. *This can't be good.* Nerves racked her system and she tried to think of how she might get away.

Fortunately, the goblins had bound her hands in front of her, so even though her movement was restricted by the enchanted rope, she fumbled to untie the knot around her ankles. Unfortunately, it wouldn't budge. Frustrated, she winced as the ropes bit further into her wrists until little fingers moved hers out of the way and very quickly untied the knot that bound her feet. Callie smiled and said, "Thank you." The girl blushed and returned the smile with a shy one of her own. The rope fell around her feet and she used her heel to drag it toward her hands, thinking it could aid in her escape. The cart jerked to a stop and the little girl tumbled against her again. "It's okay," she whispered, noting the tremors in the child's limbs.

The girl's eyes widened as the cage opened behind Callie, who turned just as they clamped a metal shackle around her neck. "What the hell?" She dropped the rope and threw her hands up to the shackle, noting the chain attached just as the mossy brown goblin gave it a tug.

"Come along, pretty. Be a good pet, and we won't have to hurt you."

"I'm a person, not a pet," she retorted, tugging on the metal collar fruitlessly.

The goblin clucked his tongue, pulling her by the leash until she was standing on a small platform in front of a gathered crowd. There were a variety of creatures there, some who looked mostly human, like the Fae she had seen on the road, and others that definitely were not. She didn't know what to make of them, and a pit of dread settled into her stomach when she realized her opportunity for escape had been removed the second they clamped the shackle around her neck. It all reminded her of studying slave auctions in history class. *Oh shit.* Her eyes widened as the puzzle pieces fell into place. *They're going to sell me.* She tugged at the collar harder, feeling the rope biting into her bound hands, causing a small amount of blood to trickle down her forearm.

"I wouldn't do that if I were you," the goblin hissed in her ear. "You're going to make them hungry."

She froze in place, studying the faces in the crowd, and she gulped when she saw more than a few of them licking their lips. Her pulse kicked into high gear, and she saw one closer to her inhale deeply and shudder. *What the hell?* On the ride in, she had been too preoccupied with the girl to really worry, but now panic filled her veins. She was up against unknown magical creatures, and some of them were staring at her like she was one of those juicy, giant turkey legs they sold at fairs. She prayed Evin was nearby and would somehow get her out of this mess.

A large goblin with oily gray skin cleared his throat off to her left. "All right folks, we'll begin the auction with a feisty human girl. She's still pretty young, but old enough." He grinned salaciously, and a few hoots echoed from the crowd in response as he approached her. She attempted to move away, but a sharp tug on the chain yanked her to her knees. He stepped closer and inhaled deeply. "Ah, what a treat we have for you—seems this one is still pure."

How can he possibly know that? Her cheeks stained a deep crimson, and she gulped. She was in way over her head. Her eyes scanned the growing crowd, and her pulse pounded in her ears so loudly she only caught bits of the prices being thrown around. She looked away from the strange faces, tamping down the disappointment and fear burning in her gut, and she saw the little girl next to the platform with the same collar and chain attached. She looked absolutely terrified, and it struck a chord in Callie. She pasted on a brave face and mouthed, "It will be okay," as got back on her feet. She tipped her chin up defiantly, determined to stay strong for the little girl, determined to not let them see her cower. *I'll get myself out of this mess somehow.* She glared at the crowd, daring anyone else to raise their hand.

CHAPTER 20

$\mathcal{E}$VIN PUSHED THROUGH the crowded streets,
eager to question Branan and return to Callie as
quickly as possible. He knew it was a risk to leave
her in the woods, but it would've been riskier to bring her
with him. The borderlands were where the wild, unaffiliated Fae lived. While the unaffiliated Fae were fine regu-
lating their own, they weren't exactly known for their fair
treatment of humans, and the goblin market was worst of
all. He passed a stall selling teeth and a necklace of human
fingers, as if there to prove his point. The afternoon sky
was quickly bleeding into dusk by the time he reached the
other side where Branan's shop was located.

When he reached a large orange and blue tent, he
pushed back one of the drapes and stepped inside the stall.
It was filled with cages containing various creatures and
luckily was empty of customers at the moment. "Ah, Evin,
to what do I owe this honor?" A male with long black hair
smiled widely.

"Branan, good to see you again. I'm hoping you may

have some information I need."

"And here I was hoping for a personal call. It's been a while." His smile remained, but a flicker of disappointment passed across his face. "Has your king been keeping you busy?"

"He has."

"And is Reid here with you? I haven't heard from him since the last time you two came to visit. He snuck out in the middle of the night, but fortunately for him, I like a good game of chase."

Hearing his brother's name still felt like opening a bleeding wound, his death still so fresh even though months had passed. Evin felt horrible admitting he had initially been too lost in his own grief and need for revenge to notify Branan. Then serving his punishment had kept him away, and now, when that should have come first, he had been so focused on getting back to Callie. He sighed, not wanting to be the one to tell his brother's on-again, off-again lover of his untimely death.

Branan's smile dropped, and he placed a hand over his heart as he took in Evin's shift in mood. "No." His voice cracked on the broken plea.

"I'm so sorry to be the one to tell you…"

"How?" His word was sharp and straight to the point.

"There was an altercation with another Fae, the Unseelie prince."

Branan hissed and guilt churned in Evin's gut, eating away at him. No matter how hard his father and the others had tried to convince him otherwise, he knew Reid's death was his fault. He was the one who had started the fight. Reid had died protecting him, had given his life for him. He would carry the weight of that single decision for the rest of his days.

Branan stepped around the counter and clasped a hand on Evin's shoulder. He had always been perceptive of others' emotions, making Evin wonder briefly if Branan was part Incubus. Branan studied Evin, his anger melting away, replaced with grief and understanding. "He loved you dearly. He would've done anything for you, and if he gave his life for yours, it was because he wanted you to live."

Evin nodded and wiped away a stray tear. Branan's words meant more than he could admit. "Thanks."

Branan cleared his throat, changing the subject and his mood just as quickly. Evin didn't fault him for wanting to push the grief away until later where it could be processed in privacy. "So, what information can I help you with?"

"It seems a quanlier has made its way into the human realm. The king has sent me to track the beast and destroy it, but I'm a little more interested in how it got there in the first place."

"Hmm…a quanlier. Those are rare and hard to control—it takes some powerful magic. Can't say I've had any of those come into my possession lately."

"Do you know of anyone who might have one or how one may have gotten loose in the human realm?"

"Well, I can tell you they're not native to any of the areas surrounding the gateways, so it would be extremely unlikely that one just wandered through on its own. I haven't met one in person, but I've heard stories of a bloodline that could control them and send them out to do their bidding."

Evin sighed. *Reid probably got his information from Branan.* "That's what I feared. A wild quanlier is one thing, but one that's following orders…well, that complicates things."

"Because now you not only have to find the beast, but also whoever controls it."

Evin nodded. "Any suggestions on where to start?"

"Quanliers are not my specialty, but there is someone around here who deals with them. Go to The Ring and ask for Niall. Tell him I sent you, and he should be able to provide you with the information you seek…for a little coin, of course."

"Thanks, Branan." Evin turned to leave, eager to return to Callie.

"Oh, and Evin." Branan paused, swallowing hard. "I'm sorry for your loss."

The words struck him like an arrow, and he stumbled, turning back to face him. Unshed tears glimmered in Branan's eyes. Evin wasn't sure why he lived out there in the borderlands with the wild Fae. He seemed too good for this place—too kind. *I can see what Reid saw in him.* "I'm sorry for yours as well. He cared about you, you know?"

Branan smiled weakly. "As much as one can care about someone when his first love is duty to his family and his king."

Evin remembered the last time he and Reid were there, how he had asked his brother about his relationship with Branan, asked him if he would ever settle down. Reid had laughed the question off with a shrug, joking that no one would be there to keep Evin out of trouble or fill their father's shoes and saying he couldn't imagine living in the borderlands. Still, Evin had been able to see the longing in his eyes, as if Reid was torn between his desires and his duty.

Evin wasn't sure how to respond, so he nodded and walked out the door, determined to check in on Branan from time to time for Reid's sake. He turned to the left, continuing the winding path deeper into the maze of tents, and then he came upon a crowd. He usually avoided this side of the market, knowing what sorts of unsavory activities went on there, but it was the quickest path to The Ring. It appeared the auction was well underway because the bids that were being thrown out were already climbing high.

"Come on, sweetheart, why don't you tell the crowd your name?" He heard the auctioneer's voice boom over the crowd. "Not that it will matter to some of them," he added with a soft chuckle, using a strategy Evin knew was used to increase fear in the humans or lesser Fae on the auction block.

He was edging his way around the crowd when she spat, "Screw you," and he froze. His head jerked toward the sound of her voice, his heart caught in his throat. Callie stood on the auction block. She had blood smeared across her forehead and a fiery defiance in her eyes. He growled, shoving his way toward the auctioneer.

"She is mine, and she is not for sale!" he yelled, a shocked hush settling over the spectators.

"I beg to differ, sir. It appears that she is," the auctioneer retorted, turning to face two other goblins at the edge of the platform with the next two victims.

"She wasn't collared when we found her," the brown one asserted.

"No brand or necklace either," the green one added.

He growled. He kept his eyes off of Callie, afraid of what he might do to the goblins if he took the time to think about her being injured and shackled by those creatures. "I left her with my dagger. I'm sure you must have seen it and the crest at the bottom." One of the two goblins swallowed and looked at the other. "As such, you know who I work for."

"Aye, but she still had no collar, no necklace, and no brand, so we're well within our rights to auction her off today. If you want her back, you'll have to buy her."

Evin narrowed his eyes, but he knew the goblin was technically acting according to borderland law. If he were to take her by force, it would upset the balance. He ground his teeth.

"Fine, I'll double whatever the leading bid is, and you'll return my dagger." He stared down the crowd and the goblins, daring anyone to object or attempt to outbid him. Thankfully, no one did.

The auctioneer stomped his foot loudly. "Sold!"

It was then that he made eye contact with Callie, and it almost brought him to his knees. There were tear tracks down her dirt- and blood-smeared cheeks, and she whimpered like a little girl when he approached.

"Unshackle and untie her right now!" he barked at the green goblin after she practically fell off the platform into his arms. The creature hobbled over with a key and unlocked the shackle around her neck as Evin gently tugged at the ropes around her wrists to loosen them until they fell to the ground. He hissed when he saw the rope burn and raw, bloodied skin underneath. He could feel her shaking and crying silently.

He stroked her hair and held her head against his chest. "Shhh, *mo rua*, I've got you now. You're safe." She nodded her head, and he wanted more than anything to ease her panic, to get his sarcastic, feisty girl back. "We'll get some salve for your wounds in a few moments." He turned his attention to the goblin and ground his teeth to keep from maiming him. "My dagger," he demanded. It was hard to release his arm from around her even just to retrieve his weapon. "Can you walk?" he whispered in her ear, and she nodded. After sliding the blade back into his belt, he wrapped one arm around her waist. "Come on, sweetheart. Let's get you out of here."

"Next up, we have a half-breed Djinn, if I'm not mistaken. A tiny thing, great for labor or housework. Perhaps someday she may even be able to grant you a wish." The announcer's voice boomed across the crowd, and Callie stopped moving.

"Wait!" She turned to the platform and then looked back at Evin with wide, pleading eyes. "I can't leave her there. We have to buy her."

He furrowed his brow. "What are you talking about? I'm not made of money, sweetheart, and you already cost me quite a bit today." He smiled at her, thinking she might rise to his teasing.

"Please," she begged, her voice raw, her eyes full of tears. "I can't just leave her. I told her it would be okay." He stared into her beautiful hazel depths and knew he would do just about anything to see her smile again.

He sighed and raised his hand, throwing out a bid. He gazed over at the auction block to see what about this girl had captured Callie's devotion, and he had to admit she looked rather pathetic. Her tiny pale blue frame was trembling as she stood up there, and he was surprised she wasn't crying. Her knees knocked together as someone else threw out a higher bid.

Callie didn't hesitate before she grabbed Evin's elbow and pushed his hand into the air. He rolled his eyes and called out an even higher amount then narrowed his eyes at his competitor and fingered the dagger at his waist intentionally. The other Fae received the threat and wisely chose not to bid again.

"I wouldn't pay that much for a *leathfuil* anyway," the other Fae said as he spat onto the ground.

Evin bit his tongue, holding in his retort. He despised those who hated half Fae for simply being born. It made him glad Callie had talked him into buying the girl, because he didn't want to think about what might have happened to her if the other Fae had won. He pulled Callie by the hand as they went to collect her.

"I'd suggest getting them collars if you want to keep them this time." The green goblin smirked, the mischievous twinkle in his eye hinting that he might find them later to see if his advice had been taken. Evin knew it was risky to have them there without anything showing they belonged to someone, but he also knew Callie would probably throw a fit if he tried to put a collar on her. He shoved the coins into the goblin's hand and turned to see the little girl clinging to Callie's leg. *At least it doesn't look like she'll run away.*

He guided them out of the crowd, keeping an eye on both girls until they turned down a side street. He led them through the winding market until he found a stall selling what he needed.

"Oh hell no! Don't even think about it," Callie threatened, pulling her hand from his grip.

The vendor stared at them curiously as Evin pushed her over to the side of the street where they were a little more secluded. "Listen, Callie, this isn't ideal for me either, but I have a feeling those goblins will find us later, and if you're not marked in some way, they will take you again. I can't risk that. This will keep you safe."

She studied his expression and read the sincerity in his eyes. "Fine, but that doesn't mean I have to like it."

"I know, and feel free to complain all you want when we're not in public."

It was only then that she noticed the other Fae staring at them curiously, watching everything unfold. She nodded, and Evin turned his attention back to the vendor, pulling her behind him.

Evin studied the collars on display along with a few branding rods. He shied away from those immediately, finding the entire practice utterly barbaric. There was a wide assortment of collars from metal to leather, some jeweled, some padded, and others studded with spikes. Some looked painful and others just uncomfortable. He couldn't imagine putting one of those around Callie's neck. He would despise it every second he had to look at it. That was when he noticed the small case of claiming necklaces. "How much for that one?" he asked, gesturing toward a golden necklace with a teardrop-shaped silvery-gray stone resembling the inside of geode.

The vendor raised one eyebrow. "Interesting choice." Evin was actually a little surprised himself to find claiming necklaces at this stall and not just collars, knowing the borderland Fae's views on humans.

"Just tell me how much."

"Six silver."

"I'll give you five. Do you have anything smaller for a child?" he asked, motioning toward the Djinn girl.

"Only plain collars, but I could stamp some flowers into one of the leather ones…for an extra fee, of course."

Evin sighed. "Are any of the leather ones soft or padded?" He hated to think of something digging into the young girl's skin and causing her discomfort.

The man scanned a case before sliding out a tray and

plucking a white strap of leather lined with soft fur, a kind usually used by nobles on their household servants. "I could cut this one down…for an—"

"Extra fee. Yeah, I got it. How much for both?"

"Ten silver."

"Eight and it's done." He reached into a small leather bag in his pocket and handed the vendor eight silver coins. The man took the white collar over to a little station, cut off the extra length, and hammered a pretty floral design into the leather.

"Pleasure doing business with you," the vendor replied as he handed both items to Evin in exchange. Evin snorted and turned his attention back to the girls. Callie was silently observing everything, and the girl was staring down at her feet. He motioned for Callie to turn around, and when she complied, he draped the necklace and closed the clasp. Stepping back, he studied her reaction.

"It's…beautiful…not what I was expecting," she said quietly. "But will it have the same effect as a collar?" She looked over his shoulder at the assortment of collars in the stall.

He nodded, unable to tell her it would actually have a greater effect. It was an older tradition, one not commonly practiced these days. The claiming necklace indicated to other Fae that she was his consort, not his slave. He hoped she didn't notice the blush that crept up his neck and onto his cheeks.

He approached the little girl next, squatting down to her level. "Hey there, beautiful. My name is Evin, and we're going to get you back to your home, okay?" Her turquoise eyes met his and he could see the questions swirling in them, but the tension in her limbs eased a bit, and she lessened the white-knuckle grip she had on Callie's hand.

"I have a necklace for you, too, but it's not as pretty." He wasn't sure how to continue, didn't know if she even knew collaring her would indicate to others that she was someone's property. It didn't help that she had yet to say a single word. "Can I put this on for you?" he asked.

Her grip on Callie's knuckles tightened, and Callie winced. She leaned down to the little girl. "It's okay. He's my friend. We're going to take care of you and get you back to your family, but you have to wear the necklace so those goblins can't come back and steal you away again."

She trembled but gave a little nod, so Evin fastened the collar around her neck. "Is it okay? Too tight? I tried to get one that wouldn't rub." She shook her head. "Does she talk?" he whispered after he stood back up.

Callie shook her head. "Not a word yet. She's probably pretty traumatized. I hope she'll trust us soon, though, or getting her back to her family will be next to impossible."

Now that both the girls were claimed, the stares weren't quite as frequent, but they were still there as they wandered through the market. Evin stopped abruptly, knowing he couldn't take either of them where he needed to go next. It was too big of a risk; too many things could go wrong.

He sighed. "What am I going to do with the two of you? It's not as if I can take you with me to The Ring." He was more or less thinking aloud, so he was slightly taken aback when he heard Callie's indignant reply.

"And why not?"

A woman passing them on the street gasped at Callie's audacity, her eyes studying them closely to see Evin's reaction.

"Not here," he hissed under his breath, steering her down a side street by the elbow, somewhat forcefully. He needed to get them somewhere safe where he could explain things better, and at the moment there was only one place that came to mind. He pulled her along behind him, retracing his steps back to the familiar orange and blue tent. As they walked, he snuck glances at the two of them. Callie walked with her head held high, observing everything, while the girl clung to her hand, her eyes downcast, and every so often reached up to tug at her collar. He hated even putting the thing on her, but leaving her unclaimed was not an option.

The girl looked to be about the same age his little sister would have been. An ache settled in his chest at the reminder of what could have been. He hadn't thought about his mother and sister since Reid's burial ceremony. He hoped they'd all found each other on the other side.

Childbirth was always risky business for Fae. It was common for something to go wrong that no magic could fix. Some thought it to be the balancing factor for their long life spans. Usually the mother would give her life to save the child's, but in some cases, as it was with his mother, both mother and child did not survive. In his sister's honor, he made a silent vow to safely return the girl to her family.

He threw back the flap to Branan's tent and stepped inside.

"Evin! I didn't expect—" Branan gaped, his eyes widening as Callie stepped in behind Evin, but he quickly schooled his features. When his eyes landed on her necklace, a smirk played at the corners of his lips. "Well, hello." He smiled at her, but his features quickly darkened as he caught sight of the little Djinn clinging to Callie's hand. "Eshna! What are you—?"

He didn't have time to get the words out before the little girl ran to him and flung her arms around his legs, holding on to him for dear life. She started sobbing and talking at the same time, which made it difficult to understand her. "Shh, shh, Eshna. Calm down. It's okay now. You're okay." Branan bent down and picked her up, wrapping her in his arms and whispering soothing words into her hair.

"I take it you know our little friend here." Relief filled Evin, knowing they now had information that could lead them to her home.

"I do. Her mother does business with me from time to time. Last I saw them was when I delivered an owl griffin for her birthday about four months ago." He turned his attention back to Eshna. "And how is your little pet doing? Did you find him a name yet?"

Eshna sniffled, a small smile cresting her lips. "I named him Bran after you!"

"Did you now?" He chuckled. "I'm honored. I'm sure Bran misses you. What happened? How long have you been gone?"

She bit her lip, thinking. "Two days. I was playing with Bran outside when he ran off into the woods. I think he saw a mouse. They're his favorite. I went after him but couldn't find him, and then…and then…" Her voice trembled and she started crying again.

"Shh, it's okay. It's all over now. We'll get you home tomorrow. I'm surprised your mom hasn't been by yet looking for you. Where did you find her?" He pulled his gaze from the little girl back to Callie and Evin.

"Goblin slave auction," Evin replied tightly.

"She was in the cage when I was captured, poor thing. None of the other prisoners would help her, but I just couldn't leave her there, so I made sure Evin bought her too."

"Bought her too?" He quirked an eyebrow at Evin.

"Yes, well, it seems leaving Callie in the woods outside of town wasn't such a good idea. I thought she would be safer, but…you can see how well that turned out. I'm just glad I happened to be walking by the market when I did." He squeezed Callie's hand, thankful she was still allowing him to hold it. "After I won her and my dagger back"—he growled lowly, his tone threatening retribution—"she demanded I also win the little girl and return her to her family, so here we are."

Branan put Eshna down, and she tugged on her collar. "Can I take this off now, please?"

Branan clenched his jaw and glared at Evin, opening his mouth to speak, but Callie knelt down next to Eshna. "Remember what we said about the goblins?" The little girl nodded. "We have to keep these on until we leave the market. We don't want those mean goblins to come back and try to take us again."

Eshna shook her head vehemently. "No, no goblins."

Evin shrugged sheepishly. "I tried to get the most comfortable one I could for her. I didn't want to claim either of them, but one of the goblins threatened to steal them back if they weren't marked. I couldn't risk that."

Branan nodded. "I understand, but I don't like it."

Their quiet was interrupted as Callie blurted, "What's a *leathfuil*?" She drug the word out hesitantly so it sounded more like *la-fool*. The little girl grimaced, as did Branan. "I'm sorry, I didn't realize—"

Evin cut in. "It's okay. It's just not a very pleasant word. It's a derogatory term for half Fae, literally meaning half-blood."

"Like calling a wizard a mudblood?"

Evin furrowed his brow, trying to work out the reference, and Branan chuckled. "That's exactly it, my little Potterhead." The crease between Evin's eyebrows deepened as Branan elbowed him in the side playfully. "Don't mind my friend here. I don't think he's as up to date on his human culture references as he believes."

"Hey! I brushed up during my last visit," he argued.

His words were like a bucket of ice water on her skin. His last visit to the human realm was the first time they met. She remembered talking to him about many things like shows and movies, but he'd claimed where he'd lived before was so rural they didn't have a movie theater and his parents didn't believe in television. She'd joked about him being Amish, and now having seen what it was like in the Fae realm, she realized it wasn't that far off. She didn't open herself up to many people, especially not to boys after everything that had happened with her father, but there was something about Evin that made her want to trust him. They had talked every day for hours, and even though they had been dating for less than a month, he had snuck past her defenses, and her carefully erected walls had started to crumble. She released his hand and took a step away, reminding her foolish heart that even though he had come to her rescue, he was still the boy who'd lied to her, the boy who had broken her heart. She couldn't afford to let him in again. Her heart wouldn't survive it.

He frowned and stared down at his empty fingers, unsure of where he had gone wrong. Branan's eyes softened as they sized her up. It felt almost as if he could see right through her, and she wondered if he was a mind reader.

"So, you can give us directions to Eshna's home?" Callie asked. "We'd like to return her to her parents."

"You're going to take me home?" Her little voice was

so full of hope and longing it made Callie's chest hurt.

"Of course we are, sweetheart. Don't you miss your mommy and daddy?"

Eshna's turquoise eyes watered and her little lip trembled before she burst into tears, and Branan lifted her into his arms to comfort her.

"I...I..." Callie was at a loss for words.

Branan pressed a hand over Eshna's ear as he spoke. "It's not your fault. Her father passed away last year, and she's been having a tough time adjusting."

"I'm so sorry, Eshna. We'll get you home to your mommy. I promise."

Branan's eyes flickered over to Evin. A promise was not something the Fae took lightly due to the magic bindings associated with those words. If they made a promise, they were bound to honor it. Evin nodded once to acknowledge her words, and Branan smiled gratefully.

Callie stuck out her pinky, and the little Djinn turned her head toward her, her eyes full of questions. "Where I come from, when we promise, we link our pinky fingers together. The pinky swear is the most sacred of promises. I, Callie, promise to return you home to your mother and your little Bran." The little girl reached out her own pinky, and Callie linked the two together. A giggle escaped Eshna as she shook their linked hands up and down. Callie smiled.

"I can see why you chose the necklace for this one," Branan murmured to Evin.

Callie reached up and fingered the pendant. "Why—"

"So, I was wondering if the girls could stay here while I follow that lead at The Ring?" Evin avoided Callie's gaze as he spoke.

"Of course. You're all welcome to stay as long as you like. I'll close up shop and you guys can stay at my place tonight."

"Thank you, I would appreciate that," Evin replied.

"Hold up! You are not just leaving me here with someone I just met." She turned to Branan with a mumbled, "No offense," before continuing, "I'm going with you."

Evin rubbed his hand across his face. "Callie, I already told you this is not a place you'd want to go, and I can't focus on getting the information I need if I'm worried about protecting you."

She thrust a hand on her hip and arched an eyebrow. "Do I need to remind you what happened the last time you left me alone?"

He sighed as Branan slapped him on the back. "She does have a point there, mate."

"Fine, you can come with me, but you have to swear you will follow my directions. You cannot question me on this. I need your complete obedience."

Callie balked at that word. She wasn't one to follow orders blindly, but if it meant she wouldn't be left behind, she was willing to give it a try. While Branan seemed like a pretty stand-up Fae, the fact remained that he was still a Fae, and she didn't trust him. She glared at Evin a few moments longer to let him know how much she didn't like either option. "Fine," she eventually grumbled.

"We'll return for Eshna when we're done." Evin addressed Branan with a nod as if all matters were settled.

"Probably best if you rest at my place before heading out, especially with this one in tow." Branan tipped his head toward Eshna, who was losing her battle to stay awake as she clung to him.

Evin took a deep breath. He had been hoping this would be a short visit. He didn't relish the idea of staying in the borderlands with Callie, but a night's rest would do them all good. While he could go on very little sleep, he didn't think the girls could. "Thank you, Branan."

"Do you remember where my home is located?"

Evin nodded in reply.

"We'll be back soon, baby girl, I promise," Callie said, holding her pinky out to Eshna, who lazily hooked her own around it before yawning loudly. She nodded sleepily.

Callie focused on Branan like a mama grizzly assessing if her cub was safe. "She probably needs to be fed before you put her to bed. Even though she's tired, I don't know the last time she ate, and those monsters sure didn't feed her."

"I'll take good care of her," Branan replied with an amused smirk.

"All right Bilbo Baggins, let's go see this ring of yours," Callie tossed over her shoulder as she walked toward the exit.

Puzzled, Evin quirked his head at Branan, who laughed and smiled as he said, "I really like her."

Evin sighed as he caught up to Callie in the blink of an eye.

CHAPTER 21

THE RING LOOKED nothing like she'd thought it would. They approached the small, stained, brown tent in a dark alley, the flickering light of the lanterns and large guard posted by the entrance like a bouncer at a club making the place appear all the more menacing. She craned her neck up to study the imposing figure. He had to have been well over ten feet tall with large muscles and a permanent scowl on his face. His large pointed ears stood out farther than a regular Fae, and with his fangs, his underbite was all the more alarming. "Password?" he grunted.

"Branan sent me. I need to speak to Niall."

The guard raked his eyes over the pair of them, widening a tiny fraction as they grazed her necklace. "Password?" he repeated in the same monotone growl.

Evin sighed, pulling out a few coins from his pocket and pressing them into the bouncer's hand. He gave a slight nod before stepping to the side and allowing them to pass without a word.

Evin pushed back the flap of the tent, reaching behind him to grab Callie's hand in a tight grip.

"And he was...?" She knew he had to be something different to be that huge.

"Troll. Keep walking."

She inhaled sharply as her eyes adjusted to the scene around her. The sketchy establishment was huge on the inside. She tried to wrap her mind around how a simple tent could hold a small auditorium. "Magic," she guessed aloud and felt Evin squeeze her hand.

"You must not be afraid. No matter what you hear or see, push the fear as far down as it can possibly go. We don't want to draw unwanted attention to ourselves."

She swallowed hard, taking several deep breaths to steady her racing heart. It didn't help that the crowd they were weaving through was composed of creatures she had never seen the likes of before. Some were tall and intimidating like the guard outside, others short but dangerous like the goblins she had already encountered. They had a wide range of skin and hair colors and features. The only thing they had in common was their loud shouting and the bloodlust in their eyes, which were focused on whatever lay at the bottom of the steps in the center ring. Evin kept her behind him, shielding her from whatever the crowd was cheering for as they walked down the stone steps and skirted the outermost ring of stone. A few Fae jumped up from their seats along the edge, yelling in an unfamiliar language as they passed behind, and thankfully their attention remained on whatever was happening below.

Suddenly a scream pierced the air, causing her to throw her hands over her ears and freeze in place. It was like the high-pitched scream of a rabbit, only with the volume turned up so high it made her head ache. Her vision swam and Evin stood in front of her, speaking, but she couldn't hear him over the ringing in her ears. She was certain he was most likely cursing or lecturing her about how she should have stayed behind. He pulled her into his chest and rubbed her hair to soothe her. She dropped her hands, the ringing in her ears yielding to the raucous cheering of the crowd.

An announcer's voice boomed over the din. "Victory to the adjule! That marks the end of this round. Ladies and gentlemen, make sure you place your bets before the next fight begins!"

"We need to find Niall," Evin whispered.

"I'm okay," she assured him, retreating from the comfort of his arms. He studied her face for a moment before nodding and resuming their search with a tight grasp on her hand. He approached a broker stand taking bets on the next fight.

"Where's Niall?" he asked.

The broker, a dark-skinned Fae with pink eyes, nodded vaguely down toward the ring where the announcer stood overseeing cleanup. Callie's stomach turned when she saw the mangled body of some creature being removed, silver blood smearing across the floor as they dragged it away. Another Fae led a snarling wolf-like creature with a silver-stained muzzle, reddish blue skin, and webbed feet toward a tunnel on the other side of the ring. *That must be the victor—the adjule.*

"What is this place?"

Evin sighed, having hoped to avoid this conversation, but there was no way around it now. "It's where people place bets to watch Fae creatures fight to the death."

"Like cockfighting? Where people gamble on rooster

fights?"

"Yes, I suppose that's a pretty good comparison, only these are dangerous creatures, not birds."

"Have you ever been chased or bitten by a goose or come across an ostrich at one of those drive-through animal parks?" she asked, trying to take her mind off the horrific scene. She never could tolerate the mistreatment of animals, always having to change the channel when those sad commercials about abused animals came on.

"Can't say that I have." The corners of his mouth tipped up, relieved to see her humor returning even though he knew she was using it as a defense mechanism. He much preferred her snark and sarcasm to her fear.

"Then just trust me then when I say birds can be pretty dangerous."

She stared at the floor as they moved, willing her eyes not to take in the gruesome sight below. When they reached the sawdust-covered floor—likely set up to soak up any blood during the fights—Evin pulled her toward the announcer. He was about Evin's height with a brown goatee and brown eyes, but what stood out to Callie was his hat, a rusty red bowler topped with a deeper crimson shade as if the top were wet with some sort of liquid. Callie shuddered internally.

"Niall?" Evin asked as they approached, shielding Callie with his body.

"Who's asking?"

"Branan sent me, said you could help me with some information."

The man looked Evin up and down, observing the pair of them as if to determine if they were worth his time. "My time isn't cheap, but Branan wouldn't send you to me if he you couldn't pay, so what can I help you with?"

Evin took the hint and fished out a few silver coins from his pouch, handing them to Niall before asking his question. "What can you tell me about quanliers? More specifically, do you know of any Fae who can control them?" he added in a lower pitch.

"Quanliers, huh? I don't really deal in 'em—too unpredictable, that bunch. I have heard some stories, though, tales of Fae who possess a unique ability to control them, to bend them to their will."

Evin slipped Niall another coin. "What can you tell me about them?"

"It's something with their magic, something in their blood that makes them able to do it. They can control most Fae creatures, make them do their bidding. It's a very rare ability that has mainly stayed within one or two families that I've heard of. My grandfather used to tell me of a girl who lived near his village when he was growing up, said one day when she was being picked on by some of the kids, a flock of birds dove out of the sky and pecked them, almost like they were protecting the girl. After it happened, the girl's family suddenly left town."

"This girl, does she have a name?"

Niall arched an eyebrow and held his hand out expectantly. Evin handed him a gold coin, so he answered, "Deryn."

"Do you know what happened to the family?"

"Why all the questions about quanliers and Dyr?"

"Dyr?" Callie wondered, unaware that she'd spoken the words aloud.

"Fae who can talk to and control beasts, a very rare thing indeed. And who might you be, poppet?" Niall leaned around Evin's frame to get a good look at her. "Not a great place for someone of your frail constitution, unless…" He appraised them both, his gaze lingering on her necklace and Evin's protective stance. "Ah, someone has it out for your girl then? Sent a quanlier after her?"

Beware the lover scorned. The words from the note bounced around in her mind. Evin growled, not caring for Niall's blunt tone.

Niall clucked his tongue. "No use taking your anger out on me, boy. I'm the one with the information, in case you forgot, and if a quanlier is after your girl, if it's had a taste of her"—Evin growled again, but Niall ignored it— "there's only one solution. You have to kill it, and in order to do that, you'll need a special kind of weapon."

Evin, already aware of what Niall was after, placed yet another coin into his greedy palm. Niall rubbed his thumb over it. "There's a blacksmith in the market, sells mostly house goods, but he has some items he keeps in the back for special customers. Look for the stall with a blue forge on the sign. Tell him Niall sent you and that you need to dispose of a quanlier. He'll have what you need."

"How do you know all of this?" Callie asked, letting her curiosity get the best of her.

"When you deal in deadly creatures, you make it your business to know. Now, I have another match to announce, and I really don't think this is one you want her to see. Best of luck to you." He winked then turned his back on them and his attention to the ring, where two handlers were waiting in the wings of the tunnels to bring out the next creatures. A dragon-like roar echoed through the stadium as the crowd got on their feet. Evin said something she couldn't hear over the ruckus and steered her through the crowd toward the exit as quickly as he could.

Once they were out in the cool, night air, he spoke again. "We'll need to find the blacksmith."

"Do you think he's still open?"

He smirked. "We're in the night market, sweetheart—everything is open until dawn."

"Well, *excuse* me for being an ignorant human," Callie huffed.

Evin closed his eyes and took a breath. "Come on, Cal. You know I didn't mean it like that."

She poked a finger into his chest. "*You* don't get to call me Cal. Now, let's go find this blacksmith so we can be done with all this nonsense."

He glanced around, thankful the only one to see her attitude toward him was the bouncer, who shot him an unexpected sympathetic glance with a slight shake of his head. Evin grabbed Callie's hand and led her through the market, grateful she didn't protest.

He located the stall Niall had described. A wizened Fae who looked like he belonged in a biker gang greeted them with a brief nod as Evin approached the counter. Callie fingered a set of silverware, admiring its intricate designs while Evin spoke. "Greetings, I'm looking for something special. Niall said you might be able to help."

The blacksmith continued to stare at them with the best poker face Callie had ever seen.

"Look, we have a quanlier problem. Can you help or not?" She had no patience for the small talk and cut right to the chase. She wanted to get back to her life.

Evin's eyes widened, certain Callie's mouth would get them both killed.

Instead, the old man's eyes softened, and he grinned. "I

like you, young lady. I have just the thing." He reached behind the counter and slid out a large metal footlocker. After some digging around, he pulled out a sword covered with a scabbard. He offered it to her handle first, and when she gripped it, he removed the scabbard to reveal a long, sharp, silver blade edged in iridescent purple. "Silver imbued with wolfsbane. Careful not to cut yourself with it, but that should take care of your beastie." The sword was heavy in her hand. She didn't think she could hold it for an extended length of time, let alone swing and thrust. She slid it back into the scabbard and passed it over to Evin, who lifted it as if it weighed nothing. The blacksmith frowned.

"How much?" Evin asked.

"Can the quanlier track her?"

Evin stared at the old man, trying to figure out why he was asking, and was surprised to see concern etched in the corners of his eyes. He nodded. The blacksmith bent over to dig around in his footlocker some more before pulling out a small dagger in a thin leather sheath with a strap and buckle. He handed it to Callie. Now this was something she could handle.

"30 piece for the both," he replied.

"And for just the sword?" Evin knew he'd pay the price for both but wanted to see why the blacksmith had handed Callie the dagger.

"Not an option. She needs to be able to protect herself. It's 30 for both, take it or leave it."

"I'll take it," Evin replied, once more reaching into his pouch to hand over coins.

"Why do you care if I can protect myself? You are aware I'm human, right?"

The blacksmith chuckled. "No use hiding what you

are, as my momma used to say, but you, my dear, put a whole new spin on that. Let's just say you remind me of someone, and if she were here now, she'd want me to help you." He smiled kindly as she cinched the dagger holster above her knee.

Evin slid the man his payment. "Pleasure doing business with you, sir."

The man nodded. "Happy hunting."

CHAPTER 22

THE BRIGHT SUN shone behind her eyelids, but she was so comfy and warm she didn't want to get up. Someone poked her side. "Five more minutes, Mom," she muttered as little girl giggles filled the air and the poking resumed.

"Wake up, sleepyhead. You promised to take me back to my momma today, and it's already morning. I've been awake for a while now, but Branan said to let you sleep."

"Remind me to thank Branan later." She opened her eyes to see the little form kneeling on the bed beside her. "Besides, who wakes someone up by poking?"

More giggles. "I do, silly."

"Well, I guess that means I have to show you how I wake my younger brother up." She lunged for Eshna, tickling her as the girl's peals of laughter and squeals filled the air. Only when she squirmed away and ran out of the room did Callie take a moment to gather herself. She searched the space for her clothes, trying to remember how she'd ended up sleeping in one of Branan's shirts but coming up short. *Oh well, I'll just have to ask where they are.* They'd gotten back so late the night before (*or was it early morning?*) that everything seemed like a blur. She remembered stumbling into bed beside Eshna while teasing Evin about sleeping on the couch. She briefly wondered if Fae had pullout couches as she stumbled from the room, yawning and running her fingers through her hair.

"I have a brush if you'd like to borrow it," Branan commented as she took a seat at the table.

She yawned again. "That would actually be amazing."

"How did you sleep?"

"Good, but it would have been better if someone didn't kick me in my sleep." Callie stuck her tongue out at Eshna.

"I'm sorry," she replied sheepishly, giggling, and Callie grinned to let her know she wasn't serious.

"Breakfast?" Branan asked, passing her a plate of scones. He motioned toward two jars on the table whose contents resembled cream and jam.

"Can't say I've had a British scone with cream and jam, or would we call these Fae scones? Did you make them yourself?" She smirked, picturing Branan in an apron covered with flour.

"I had a little help." Branan smiled at Eshna.

"These aren't scones, silly. They're biscuits, and they're my favorite." Eshna smiled with glee.

Only then did Callie notice Evin's absence, and she asked where he was.

"Out gathering supplies is what he told me when he left. I'm sure he'll want to leave as soon as he returns. I have a horse and small cart you can use to take Eshna home. The horse knows his way back, and her mom can return the cart the next time they come to the market. It should only take a day's journey that way."

She nodded. *Makes sense.* She finished off the meal, making small talk as she ate. Eshna wanted to play with some of the harmless creatures in Branan's stables out back as soon as she was finished eating, excited by the prospect of making new animal friends. "Necklace first," Branan demanded, and she groaned but complied, letting Callie clasp the collar around her tiny neck.

"Just to be safe, little one. We want to get you home to your mommy," Callie told her, securing the buckle.

"And to little Bran," Eshna added.

Callie chuckled. "And to little Bran."

Branan stayed at the table, talking to Callie after Eshna left. He was very curious about her life and how she'd come to meet Evin. She wasn't sure if it was a story she wanted to share, but something about him made her open up. She couldn't help but notice how he flinched and paled when she told him the bits about Evin pretending to be his brother. His hands clenched around each other, his knuckles turning white when she revealed why Evin had been pretending. She hesitated.

"Did he say who killed him? Why he chose you?" He practically growled the words, and while she felt comfortable around Branan, there was something dark and deadly in his gaze that made her blood run cold.

"Casimir. He was apparently following a friend of mine, had become obsessed with her for some strange reason." Something in the tightening of his jaw made her unwilling to tell him about Ianthe. She knew her bestie's true identity needed to be hidden at all costs.

Not liking the direction their conversation had taken,

she quickly tried to wrap up the story. "So, once his plan backfired and I was returned home by order of the Seelie king, my memory was supposed to be erased, but the knight who returned me thought it would be better for me to learn from my mistakes."

"And yet, here you are again, in Fae." His features sharpened like a bloodhound trying to sniff out the truth amidst her lies.

She stared at the last bits of her biscuit, moving crumbs around on her plate. "Yes, well, that's not entirely my fault. With a quanlier running around my town, I probably should have stayed put in my car when it broke down, but I really didn't want to be a sitting duck, and I wasn't sure if it could claw its way into my car, especially after seeing what it can do to a person." She swallowed hard, struck by the image of Steve's body. She shook her head to rid herself of the mental picture. "Anyway, I tried to make it back to the party to call someone, but it found me. Luckily Evin was there to save me as he was tracking it, but I managed to scrape my foot while getting away."

"It has your scent?" He inhaled sharply, his voice having lost any trace of its earlier suspicion and anger.

"Unfortunately."

"You know the only way to stop it from continuing to track you is to kill it, right?"

She nodded. "That's the plan."

Branan blew out a harsh breath, and Callie had had enough of the conversation and where she was sure it was headed. "Do you know where my clothes are?"

His brow furrowed at the shift in topic. "Yes, I washed them. They're in my room with the rest of the laundry."

"Thanks. I think I'll change now." She stood as he

studied her thoughtfully, watching her retreat.

Her dress and vest were neatly folded on Branan's bed with some other clothes. She sorted through the items and blushed as she recovered her undergarments. She slipped them back on, unsure of what to do with Branan's shirt, and then she saw what looked like a few dirty garments thrown over a chair in the corner of the room. As she walked toward it, she took a moment to study his room, noting the framed photo on the dresser. There were two men; one was Branan, and one looked an awful lot like a younger version of Evin's father, whom she had met on her last trip to Fae. The man had his arm around Branan and a wide grin on his face, while Branan's faced was tilted toward his, looking at him with adoration. She placed his shirt next to the clothes on the chair, lightly fingering the buttery smooth leather vest.

"Please don't." Branan's whispered plea shattered her musings, his voice cracking with emotion.

"I'm sorry. I didn't mean to," she apologized. She wasn't sure what for exactly, but the pain in his words struck a chord in her. He closed his glistening eyes as she removed her fingers from the garment. "I wasn't sure where to put your shirt. I didn't mean to…" She still wasn't sure what she was saying sorry for.

"I know you didn't. It's just…I left them just as he did the morning he left, hoping he would return for them soon. It wasn't the first time he'd gone silent on a mission, and I didn't expect that the silence meant…" He trailed off as he swallowed thickly, walking toward the chair.

She inhaled deeply, the pieces clicking together. No wonder that man looked like Evin's father—it's a picture of his other son, Reid. The clothes strewn so casually on a chair in Branan's bedroom…oh…oh no… Her heart broke for him. "*You loved him,*" *she whispered aloud.*

He picked up the vest and brought it to his nose, inhaling the last of Reid's scent before sitting on the bed. "Very much," he replied before breaking down. He hugged the fabric to his chest as he wept.

It was perhaps the most heartbreaking thing Callie had ever witnessed. His grief was so fresh, it made her wonder if their visit was the first time he'd heard of his lover's death. *No wonder he was so upset while I was telling my story.* She wrapped her arms around him, offering what comfort she could while he grieved, and she wasn't sure how long they sat there with her arms embracing him before Evin's voice boomed from down the hall. "Branan? Callie?"

Branan wiped at his eyes, and Callie gave him one last squeeze. "I'll stall him for as long as you need. Take your time." She closed the door behind her as she walked to the living room.

"You ready?" Evin asked. "Where's Branan?"

"He's just getting dressed," Callie lied, watching Evin's lips tug down and studying the hallway from which she'd just emerged. She sighed, giving up the lie. "How long has he known about Reid's death?"

Evin paled, his lips forming a tight line.

"That long, huh?" she guessed. "He's grieving. Give him a few minutes to pull himself together, and for goodness' sake, don't let him know I told you. I swear—are all Fae this self-conscious about others seeing how they really feel? You know, it's okay to mourn someone you've lost. There can be something very therapeutic in a good cry."

"Emotions are a sign of weakness," Evin automatically replied, blushing after the words left his mouth, confirming what she'd suspected.

Sensing his discomfort, she changed the subject. "Let me grab my dagger, and we can get Eshna. Branan mentioned earlier that we could borrow his horse and cart."

Evin cleared his throat. "Yeah, I'll go get them hitched up." She watched him go, his shoulders slumped forward as if he were once again carrying the weight of the world. She wanted to lighten his burden and carry some of it for him, but she didn't think he would let her. *Besides, you're supposed to be over him*, she chided herself.

She collected her new dagger from the guestroom, strapping it to her thigh above her knee, and she made the bed before going to see if Evin needed any help. She practically ran into Branan as she left the room.

"Sorry," they both said at the same time then stood awkwardly, unsure of how to proceed.

"Thank you." Branan exhaled. "I can see why he's so taken with you." He fingered the pendant around her neck.

"It doesn't mean anything," she protested. "He just had to give me something to keep the goblins away."

"And yet he chose a claiming necklace when he could have bought you a collar, and for much less coin at that."

"What difference does it make?"

"All the difference," he replied before they were cut short by the sound of Evin's footsteps.

"We're all set. I got the cart hitched, our bags are stowed, and Eshna's ready, although she's sad to leave you and the 'beasties', as she calls them." They followed Evin out to where the horse and cart were waiting for them. "I put some straw in the back to make the ride a little more comfortable for you both."

Branan gathered Eshna into his arms, squeezing her tightly. "You be good for Callie and Evin, okay? I'll come see you soon."

"Promise?" She held her little pinky out for him to take.

He shot a quick smile at Callie before hooking his pinky around Eshna's. He placed her gently into the cart where she settled on some of the straw.

"You do realize a promise is much more serious for a Fae than a human, right?" he joked to Callie as she approached.

"It depends on the human. Some of us take our promises deadly serious."

He pulled her in for a quick hug. "Don't let anything happen to him. He's all I have left of Reid."

She pushed away the lump in her throat. "I'll keep him safe. I promise," she whispered before releasing him, and then she hopped up and settled next to Eshna.

Branan turned his attention toward Evin. "Take good care of them both."

"I will."

"And don't be a stranger. I expect to see and hear from you every now and again."

"Will do." They shook hands before doing a quick one-arm hug before Evin mounted the horse.

"Safe travels!" Branan called, waving as they pulled away.

CHAPTER 23

ALLIE THOUGHT THE market didn't seem quite as dark and forbidding in the sunlight. Of course, they choose that particular moment to pass a stall where she saw an older woman drop a human hand into a pot hanging over a fire pit, the sign above her advertising fresh meat stew. Callie turned away and entertained herself by teaching Eshna how to play rock-paper-scissors until they made their way out of town. They headed in the opposite direction from where they'd come, the woods thinning out to rolling hills of green and reminding her of the images she'd seen of Scotland. Despite all the horror she'd seen so far, she could see why some humans would choose to remain in Fae. Unsure how far this detour would take them from their final destination, she settled into a somewhat comfortable position, listening to Eshna's persistent chatter. She obviously had no trouble talking now.

They stopped now and then to relieve themselves, stretch, and eat. They were cautious of other travelers, and

Evin refused to stop when they passed through two smaller towns, his eyes constantly flicking from the road to the precious cargo in the back, trusting the horse would steer them safely through. Callie dozed in and out, same as Eshna, until the sun set behind the horizon.

The moon lit their path as they approached a small farm. The land was marked off by a low, crumbling stone wall, and a stone farmhouse with a thatched roof loomed in the distance. Callie hoped Evin knew where he was leading them. Straw poked her legs, but she was thankful for the cushion against the hard, wooden cart. The dirt road they'd traveled on had been bumpy, to say the least. Eshna stirred against her, letting out a few soft murmurs in her sleep, almost as if she could sense them drawing closer to her home. Callie ran her fingers through the girl's lavender hair, knowing how much some women would spend in a salon just to fail to achieve the gorgeous color that came naturally to some Fae.

Just as Evin pulled the cart to a stop and climbed down from his perch, a disheveled woman rushed through the door holding a hoe. He threw his hands up in a peaceful gesture before he reached over to help Callie from the cart. She held Eshna in her arms as he gripped her waist and helped her down. The woman, who hesitantly hung back in the doorframe, unsure of what to make of her nighttime visitors, dropped her weapon the minute she saw the little girl in Callie's arms.

"Eshna!" she cried in the most beautiful voice Callie had ever heard.

"Momma?" Eshna blinked up at Callie sleepily as she shifted her to the ground. "Momma!" Eshna squealed, running toward her mother, who scooped her up, hugging her tightly.

Evin glanced at Callie, his heart aching inexplicably as he watched the tears trickle down her face. She wiped at her cheeks, somewhat embarrassed by the display of emotion. He slipped his hand around hers and gave it a reassuring squeeze to let her know she wasn't the only one touched by the mother-daughter reunion. They watched the pair talking in hushed voices for several moments, the conversation punctuated by hugs and kisses before the woman lowered Eshna to the ground. The little girl gripped her mother's hand and pulled her over to introduce her to her new friends. "This is Callie and Evin," she said, as if that explained everything, and perhaps it did; after all, they hadn't been able to overhear what she'd told her mother earlier.

With one hand still clutching her daughter's, the woman pulled Callie into a fierce hug. "I'm Amani, Eshna's mom. It's wonderful to meet you both. I…" She paused, her voice thick with emotion. "I can't tell you how grateful I am to you both for bringing her home. I've been out searching every day since she went missing, scouring all nearby towns and asking for help. I've been beside myself with worry, wondering if she would show up here while I was gone. I was about to head to the goblin market in the morning, but I didn't want to consider…" She released a shakey breath, her eyes watering.

"It was no trouble, really. I'm just glad we were able to find her family. You have Branan to thank for that. He's the one who gave us directions here," Callie interjected, not wanting to give Amina time to consider the possibilities of what could have been.

"Yes, but for you to show her kindness when others would not in the midst of grave danger speaks highly of your character."

Callie blushed. "Thank you."

"And you," she said, releasing Callie and standing before Evin. "Please tell me how I can repay you."

"There's no need. It was Callie who insisted we purchase her and bring her back to her family." He shifted, uneasy with the attention and gratitude beaming in the woman's eyes. His job didn't usually entail such things. Sure, he was known for his ability to fix situations for the king, but the problems usually fell more along the lines of bounty hunting, tracking down those who stepped out of bounds or neglected to pay their taxes and bringing them before the king for judgment. He figured his task of dealing with the quanlier was another way to fix such a situation, but he was relieved to have the opportunity to earn his way back into the good graces of his king, after…

Eshna's voice broke through his thoughts. "Come meet little Bran!" She tugged on Callie's hand insistently, and Callie grinned, allowing herself to be pulled away. "You too, Evin!" Eshna called over her shoulder.

"Come here for a minute," he replied, beckoning her forward with his finger. She dropped Callie's hand and walked toward him as he knelt down. "Can you turn around? I'm going to take off your necklace now that you're safe at home." She complied and he gently removed the collar, giving her shoulder a little squeeze. "You are such a brave little girl."

"I'm not a little girl—I'm a princess." Her wide turquoise eyes stared him down, daring him to contradict her declaration.

"Is that so?" He smiled.

"Yep. Branan told me you're a Seelie knight."

"That's true…" he answered hesitantly, unsure how that made her a princess.

"And in the stories Momma reads to me, all the knights rescue princesses. Since you rescued us, that makes Callie and me princesses."

He snickered softly. "I suppose so."

She grinned. "Princess Callie, little Bran is waiting for us."

Callie observed the whole conversation, trying to ignore the pattering of her heart. Seeing the kindness he showed the little girl did weird things to her insides. Fortunately, she was saved from delving deeper into her emotions by Eshna pulling her through the front door. The room they entered was warm and cozy. The dying embers of a fire glowed in the hearth against one wall, and Amani quickly walked over, feeding the fire and placing a few fresh logs on top. A squawk drew her attention to the cutest little creature she had ever seen perched on a chair. Like a hybrid of an owling and a kitten with downy feathers blending into fur beneath its wings, the owl griffin danced on its furred paws, growing more and more excited as Eshna approached.

"Bran!" she squealed, wrapping her pale blue arms around him and stroking his feathered head down to his wings. His tail wrapped around her arm like he couldn't get enough contact with her. She brushed a small finger down his beak as he cooed happily.

Amina sighed, placing a hand over her heart. Callie could clearly see how Eshna took after her looks. The slender shape of their turquoise eyes and smile were almost identical. Amani's hair had appeared jet black under the night sky, but now as she stood near the fire, Callie could see deep purple tones glimmering in the firelight.

"Bran, this is my friend Callie. Callie, this is Bran." Eshna held her owl griffin in front of her.

"Hello Bran," Callie replied, holding her fingers up like one would when allowing a dog to get their scent. Bran nipped at her gently with his beak and then pushed his head into her palm so she was petting him. "Well, isn't he just the cutest?"

"Will you grant us the favor of staying the night and getting some rest before you continue on your journey? Eshna and I would love the opportunity to show you our gratitude." Evin glanced back at the cart. "We can unhook your horse and rest him in the stable," Amina suggested.

He sighed, knowing it was probably best for Callie to rest before they continue, and this seemed like the safest place for them to do that. "The horse and cart actually belong to Branan. I was told to leave the cart here and you could deliver it to the market the next time you went. He said the horse would find his own way back, but resting for the night does sound nice."

Callie's stomach chose that exact moment to growl loudly, and she blushed as Eshna giggled. "Sounds like someone's hungry, Momma."

"I have just the thing! Please, come sit." Amina motioned toward a table and chairs in one corner of the room. Callie and Evin sat while Eshna rushed to help her mother.

"Are you sure we're okay to stay here for the night?" Callie asked, not because she was worried about her own safety, but more out of concern that the more time they spent in Fae, the longer she was away from the human world.

"Yes. Even though we now have the means to kill the quanlier, it won't do us much good unless we find out who sent it and why."

Callie fingered the crumpled note in her pocket, pulling it out and handing it over to him. Evin smoothed out the scrap and read it, his brow furrowing.

"Where did you get this?" The note dropped from his fingers onto the table between them.

"Do you know what it means?" she asked.

He shook his head.

"It was in the pocket of the vest you gave me. I wasn't sure what it meant or if it was even meant for me."

He sighed. "Alyss."

"Alyss as in the friend's wife who gave us the clothes and food? Or is there another Alyss I should know about?"

Evin smirked. *Jealousy looks good on her.* "The former. She's also a seer of sorts. She'd had a vision the morning I gathered supplies and wasn't feeling well enough to meet with me." His lips pressed into a tight line, knowing exactly why this was now in their possession.

"So, this was meant for me." Callie fingered the note, drawing it closer to her. "Or you."

"Probably you, or both of us, I think—though I don't know anyone from my past who might be a Dyr."

Callie scowled, not wanting to think about how many girls may have been in his past. "Well, it's not like I've dated any other Fae, so it must mean one of yours. You might want to think a little harder." She narrowed her eyes at him, daring him to contradict her.

"We'll need to ask around. If we can track down Deryn's relatives, it'll lead us in the right direction. Surely someone will have heard of this Fae."

"You truly can't think of any of your lovers the note may refer to?"

He sighed. "It's not like there's been a plethora of women, Callie."

She didn't want to admit how his words warmed her, so instead she steered the conversation in a different direction. "And who do you intend to ask about Deryn?"

He swallowed, knowing she was not going to like his answer. "The best place to start would be with the most people I could ask, which would be…"

She sighed. "Back in your town." She swallowed as her gut churned. She had hoped they would be returning to her world by now. "And the risk involved?"

"Is no higher than it was when we were there a few days ago. Besides, I'm willing to deal with the consequences."

She blanched, not wanting to know what those consequences may be. He'd already dealt with enough for the last time she was there. He'd never fill his brother's shoes at this rate, if that was what he wanted to do. Come to think of it, she hadn't asked him what he was going to do after she'd found out the truth. He'd left her at his house, and by the time he had returned, Conall and his father were there to order him to take her home. She knew through conversations with Ianthe and Conall that his brother was being groomed to take over his father's position when he was murdered. *Does Evin want to take Reid's place?*

His hand covering hers jerked her out of her musings, and he ran his thumb across her skin in a gentle, soothing motion. His touch warmed her, and she closed her eyes. "Don't worry, Callie. I'll keep you safe. I promise."

She swallowed, feeling the full weight and magic of that promise.

"Dinner's ready." Amina's voice cut through the intense moment. Eshna giggled, rushing from the kitchen to the table carrying a plate a bread. Amina followed behind with two bowls of stew. "It's not much, but it's my mother's recipe." She placed the bowls in front of Callie and Evin, returning with Eshna to the kitchen before they carried back silverware and two more bowls of stew. Dinner conversation flowed easily between the four of them. Eshna loved hearing stories about Callie's world, and Callie was amused to no end by Eshna's adventures with Bran. Eshna also told them stories of her father, her voice growing soft and solemn when she mentioned him.

"Do you know what the best part about family is?" Callie asked.

Eshna blinked up at her. "What?"

"That no matter what happens or where we go, we always carry them with us."

"We do?"

"Yep. They live here." Callie placed her fingertips on Eshna's forehead before moving them to her chest. "And here. We carry them forever in our memories and in our hearts. They live on as long as we remember them."

Had she taken a moment to glance over at the other two adults at the table, she would have seen Amina wiping away a few stray tears and Evin sitting very still. He was struck by her words and had unknowingly moved his own hand over his heart. She was offering more than comfort to a small girl; he knew her words were also meant for him. He fell a little harder for her in that moment and closed his eyes, swearing on his brother's memory to do whatever he could to make this girl happy, even if it meant returning her to her own world and letting her go for good.

"Momma, can Callie sleep with me tonight?" Eshna's voice broke through his thoughts and he opened his eyes. Callie was studying him. He wasn't sure how long she had been watching, but he was moved when she gently pulled his hand away from his chest and gave it a squeeze.

"That depends on Callie," Amina replied.

Callie released his hand and turned her attention back to their hosts. "I would love to, as long as someone doesn't kick me in their sleep again."

Eshna giggled while Amina's cheeks flushed. "What about Evin?" the girl asked as her mother stood and started clearing the table.

"He can take my bed."

"No, no," Evin insisted, rising to help with the dishes. He could never kick a woman out of her own bed. "The couch will be fine. Thank you."

"Are you sure?"

Callie chuckled. "We slept on the floor of a cave—I'm sure he can handle the couch, Amina. Besides, he's too much of a gentleman to let you sleep anywhere but your own bed."

"Are you sure you're okay sleeping in Eshna's bed with her? It's a little small."

Callie smiled at the gentle Djinn. "I have a younger brother who likes to crawl into my bed when he has nightmares, so I'm used to it."

"You must miss him." Amina placed a gentle hand on her shoulder and squeezed, and Callie saw Evin pause at the sink.

"Very much so. I hope to get back to him soon."

"Time for us to get ready for bed, silly." Eshna squealed, hopping up to Callie's chair and taking her hand, pulling her away from Evin and Amina.

"Say good night to Evin first, sweetheart," her mother called out.

"Oh yeah." Eshna dropped Callie's hand and ran back

toward him, and he bent down as she threw her arms around his neck. "Good night, Evin. Sweet dreams." She placed a goodnight kiss on his cheek, and he gave her one in return. Callie melted a little at the sight.

"Good night, Eshna. Sweet dreams. Take care of Princess Callie for me. Make sure she gets some sleep."

"I will," she replied before running over to her mother and repeating the goodnight ritual.

"Your turn, Callie." Eshna beckoned her over.

"But I'm going to sleep with you, silly."

Eshna shook her head. "No, it's your turn to say good night to Evin and Momma just like I did."

Callie blushed. She walked over and hugged Amina. "Good night. Thank you again for your hospitality."

"Nonsense. Let me know if you need anything." Amina returned her hug.

Callie turned toward Evin and hesitated. Being close to him was hard enough, but being directed by a child to hug and kiss him good night—well that took the cake. It was awkward until he wrapped his arms around her, and then everything felt right.

"Good night, Callie." She felt his breath whisper into her ear before his lips pressed against her cheek, warming her skin and sending tingles to her toes.

"Good night, Evin." She pulled back but stopped when she saw Eshna watching them and frowning.

"You didn't give him a goodnight kiss."

"Eshna—" her mother started, but Callie stopped her.

"Of course! How could I forget?" She leaned forward once more and kissed his cheek. She meant for it to be quick, but based on the giggles Eshna let out, she guessed she'd held it longer than she realized. She quickly stepped back, blushing.

"Okay, time for the princesses to get their beauty rest," she announced, taking Eshna's hand in her own and leading her down the hallway.

After they both washed up and she read Eshna a story, they climbed into bed. Eshna was out the moment her head hit the pillow. Callie stared at the ceiling, wondering how Evin was enjoying the couch. She sighed, unable to chide herself for thinking about him or muster up even the slightest bit of outrage toward him. She was starting to see the man he truly was, and she liked him. The only thing keeping her feet on the ground was the reminder of their differences, in age and aging, as well as in species.

In the other room, Evin lay awake on the couch, and Amina had followed the girls to bed. This would be the second time Callie slept in another room from him, and he wasn't a fan. He missed the feel of her in his arms. He hadn't slept much the night before, listening to hear if she had another nightmare and needed him in the middle of the night. Grateful she seemed to be sleeping well with Eshna, he closed his eyes and let sleep wash over him.

Chapter 24

THE SCREECHING SOUND of a kettle pulled Evin out of sleep. "I hope you like tea," Amani called from the kitchen.

He stood and walked over, noting it was still dark outside. "I do."

"Excellent. I thought you'd like an early start." She poured the hot water into two cups and added the tea, giving each cup a nice swirl with a spoon.

"Correct again," he replied with a smile.

She handed him a steaming cup and motioned toward the table, where they both took a seat. "I'd like to thank you again for returning Eshna to me. I can't even…" She paused, her throat thick with emotion, and swallowed. "I just…"

He reached over and squeezed her hand briefly, cutting off the rest of her words. "As I said last night, it was really no trouble. We were happy to be able to return her home."

"I know, and as *I* said last night, I'd like to repay you."

He opened his mouth to speak, but she put a hand up to stop him. "Before you tell me it's not necessary *again*, you took great risk in bringing my daughter back to me, not to mention the coin you spent at auction, but more than that, you returned to me that which I treasure most in this world. As is tradition with my people, I'm granting you a boon you cannot refuse—a wish. You may use this wish at any time, for anything." She took a shiny copper coin from her pocket and pressed it into his palm. The magic within the token sparked against his skin. Its weight was lighter than he expected, and the surface was engraved with a word in a language he couldn't read. "When you are ready, use the coin to summon me. Say my name as you hold it in your hand, and I will come to you immediately. Please remember, this is one wish, so use it well, and use it wisely."

He was stunned by her generosity. Djinn wishes were the greatest of honors and could not be bought or coerced out of them. They had to be given out of free will, and as such were incredibly rare. The Djinn were not fond of doling out wishes, as they were bound with their life to grant it. He rubbed the coin between his fingers before slipping it into his pouch. "Thank you, Amina. I will use it wisely."

"There are limitations, of course. I still have to follow the laws of nature and our land, as well as the will of our gods. I cannot bring back the dead, I cannot grant you more wishes, and so on. While I can grant a large fortune, I have a feeling you'll be more creative than that. It is meant to grant the true desire of your heart."

He'd have been lying if he said the thought of using magic to bring his brother back hadn't crossed his mind, even though he knew it was an impossibility. Sometimes it's hard to convince your heart something is impossible when it longs for that thing so much.

"Now, would you like something to eat before you

200

go?"

"That would be lovely," he replied.

The little body curled up against Callie made her smile as she shook off sleep. Eshna had insisted they share a bed, and who was she to refuse? With the girl next to her, she hadn't dreamed, or if she had dreamed, she didn't remember them, not like the nightmares she'd been having lately. She blinked in the dark, wondering what time it was and debating attempting more sleep before deciding it would be useless as she was already awake. She knew they had to leave early to make it back to Evin's home, and even then, it would take longer than the trip out there had considering how far they'd traveled to reach Eshna's home. She climbed out of the bed, careful not to jostle the sleeping child, and quietly crept into the kitchen, where she heard movement.

Evin sat at the kitchen table sipping something hot while Amina cooked, and he smiled when he caught sight of Callie. "Good morning. I was going to wake you when breakfast was ready."

She smiled. "I'm up, but Eshna's still out like a light. I don't blame her after the last few days she's had." She noticed the way Amina immediately stilled and wished she could swallow the words back down. The funny thing about words is you can't take them back. Once they're out, you can only move forward. "She slept like the dead, though, so that's something to be grateful for. No nightmares as far as I could tell." Amina's back was still toward her, facing the stove, but Callie saw her shoulders immediately relax as she continued cooking.

Callie took a seat at the table, hoping to not put her foot in her mouth again, and Evin squeezed her knee. She looked up at his warm, reassuring smile that told her *It's okay, you didn't mean it that way* in that silent way of his. She quickly shifted the topic. "So, what's the plan for to-day?"

"We'll head out after breakfast. I hope to make it back to the cave we stayed at the last time to rest for the night."

"But we're even farther away, and it took us practically all day yesterday just to get out here in the opposite direction."

He smirked over his cup before taking another sip. "You forget how much taking the horse and cart slowed us down yesterday. As long as we don't have to make too many stops, I'm confident I can get us there by nightfall."

"Would you like some tea, dear?" Amina's voice cut through their conversation.

"Yes, thank you." A minute later, the kind woman placed a mug of steaming hot tea on the table in front of her.

Callie lifted it to her lips, lightly blowing across the surface to make it drinkable. Once she felt like it was suf-ficiently cooled, she took a sip, and her eyes caught Evin staring at her mouth. "What?" she asked after swallowing.

He shook his head and smirked. "I didn't think you'd like tea."

"What's that supposed to mean?"

"It means I've usually seen you drink those super sug-ary fancy drinks humans like to call coffee."

"Well, my grandma is like an official tea aficionado, so drinking tea is a requirement for living in her house. Also, frappuccinos are delicious. They even make chai tea ones."

He shook his head and snickered as Amina started bringing over plates and food. "Do you want me to go get Eshna?" Callie offered, but Amina shook her head.

"I'll get her. I've missed waking her up in the mornings."

"I honestly don't know how you didn't insist on sleeping with her last night," Callie added, knowing that if something like that happened to her brother, no one would stop her from sleeping in his room to make sure he was safe.

"I'll have all week to sleep with her, and I couldn't deny her the joy of a sleepover with a new friend, but don't think that meant I didn't check on both of you constantly." The two of them shared a moment that made Callie homesick for her own mother.

As if he could read exactly where her thoughts wandered, he gave her knee another squeeze. Only then did it register that his hand had never left it from when she first sat down. Unsure of how to feel about that, she shifted, using the excuse of serving them both food to wiggle her knee out from underneath his hand. He frowned when he no longer had contact with her, and she tried to ignore it. "Tell me when," she said, scooping scrambled eggs onto his plate.

"That's good. Thank you."

She picked up another plate of meat that looked like bacon but wasn't quite. She placed some on his plate before eyeing her own. *What the hell, right? You only live once.* She added some to her own plate and took a bite, pleased as the sweet and savory flavors danced across her tongue. It tasted like a cross between pork belly and turkey bacon with a hint of maple.

She had just finished adding some biscuits and cheese to their plates when Eshna stumbled in, still rubbing the sleep out of her eyes. With her bedhead and rumpled night-gown, the little half Djinn was as precious as could be. She was unusually quiet until midway through their meal when she struck up a conversation.

"Momma, I don't want them to go. Can they stay longer?"

Amina smiled softly. "It's not up to me, my love. Besides, they have important things to do, and their own families to get back to."

"But will you come visit?" Eshna asked, blinking up at Callie with her puppy dog eyes.

Callie dramatically chewed her bite of biscuit to stall for time, and Evin jumped in. "I'll come back and visit, but Callie lives back in the human world."

"But she could stay here and live like Papa did, couldn't she?"

Ah, to be so young and innocent, so unaware of life's actions and consequences, Callie thought before answering. "If I did that, I would have to leave my mommy and little brother. I don't think that's very fair to them, do you?"

The corners of her mouth tugged down. "No, I suppose not." She crossed her arms in typical pouting fashion.

"I'll tell you what—how about you write me letters, and when Evin visits he can bring them to me, and I can send you ones back." The words were out before she thought through her offer. She probably shouldn't have volunteered something Evin would have to be responsible for carrying out, and besides, that would mean future contact with him. She almost wanted to kick her own butt for making the suggestion, but she couldn't take it back now, not when the little girl's face lit up like it was the best idea ever.

Callie glanced at Evin hopelessly. "Would that be okay with you?"

He smiled at the two girls. "Nothing would make me happier."

She wasn't sure what his reply meant. Did he mean it wouldn't be a bother, or was he happy to have an excuse to maintain contact with her?

They finished up their meal with polite conversation and repacked their bags. Amina handed them some food to take with them, for which they were incredibly thankful. She hugged Callie hard. "Thank you again for bringing my baby back to me. I'm in your debt."

Callie took a moment and a deep breath, willing herself to ask the questions she yearned to have answered. "Was it hard? Being with her dad when he was human? Knowing you would love him only to lose him?"

Amina's turquoise eyes softened with understanding. "Sometimes you can't explain love. It is its own force, and no matter how much you try to convince your heart not to succumb, there's no stopping it. Did I wish we had more time together? Of course, but we knew what would happen going into it, and if I had the chance to do it all again, I wouldn't change a thing. We loved so fiercely, and he gave me the best part of himself in Eshna. Every time I look at her, she reminds me of him and the love he had for the both of us. The hardest part was pushing away all the doubt and allowing myself to fall. After that, loving him was as easy as breathing. By the time he left this world, we had both made our peace. Besides, you never know how life will turn out. You could love someone you think you will grow old with only to lose them unexpectedly to battle or disease. You can't live too scared to love, or you're not fully living."

Callie hugged Amina once more. "Thank you."

"I hope that helps you, and for what it's worth, he looks at you the same way my William looked at me." Amina walked away, leaving those last words to settle in Callie's gut. She knew Evin cared about her, but they had been through so much. *Would he live in the human world for me? Would I live in Fae for him? Is there even hope for us?* She shoved the questions down into her gut, knowing this was not the time to ask them, not when they had bigger issues to deal with. *Once we get rid of the quanlier, I can figure it all out.*

Eshna tackled her legs, yanking her from her thoughts. "I'll miss you, Princess Callie."

"I'll miss you too, Princess Eshna." She hugged the little girl to her. "I need you to promise me something before I go."

"Momma said last night I'm not supposed to make promises to others."

"Your momma is a very smart woman, but I think in this case, she won't mind. Promise me you won't wander off from home again until your mom says you're old enough, even to follow little Bran. He's already proven he can take care of himself and return home. Stay close so your momma can keep an eye on you, okay? I don't think she can go through losing you again. Can you promise me that?"

Eshna nodded solemnly before sticking out her pinky, which Callie linked with her own.

"Good. Now, we have to get going, but maybe I'll send you back something special from my home when we get there. Would you like that?"

Of course, like any child offered a gift, Eshna nodded zealously. Callie glanced at Evin and Amina, who were watching the two of them closely. Amina mouthed, "Thank you," which lead Callie to believe they had heard the promise Eshna made. "Okay, be good," she added to the girl as she walked over to Evin.

Eshna's brow furrowed. "Aren't you going to take the horsey?"

Evin grinned widely. "Nope, the horsey needs to go back to Bran. Besides, I'm much faster." He winked at Eshna as he squatted down for Callie to climb on his back. "See you soon, Princess Eshna." He whisked them both away to the little girl's squeals of delight. Callie laughed softly, knowing the next time Evin visited, he'd probably have to give Eshna a piggyback ride. She gripped him tight and held on, taking a moment to breathe him in and calm her racing heart.

The open hillsides made their travel much faster with no trees to dodge. It also left them more exposed than Evin cared for, so he was sure to move as quickly as he could until they were hidden. A few times they had to stop to relieve themselves, eat, and let Callie stretch her legs, but she was doing much better than the first day they had traveled. As afternoon bled into evening, he could feel her grip on him loosening and switched over to carrying her in his arms. It was a little awkward to run but far safer than having her slip off of him at his speed, and they made it to the cave a little past nightfall.

He collected firewood while Callie refilled their water

pouch by the stream, keeping her in his sights as much as possible. When he got a fire going, they sat and cooked some fish he'd caught for dinner. Over the course of their meal, he made small talk with her, asking about her family and future plans beyond school. Knowing her plans didn't include him was a hard pill to swallow. He sighed.

"Am I boring you?" she asked.

"No."

Callie shifted nervously. He longed to ask if she could ever imagine living in a place like Fae, but it wasn't fair of him to ask, especially not when things between them were so uncertain. There'd been a time he'd thought she could never forgive him, but recently, the way she looked at him was more like it had been when they were dating. He missed that connection with her and found himself touching her more frequently, unable to resist the call of her skin and the comfort he took in her warmth. She didn't immediately reject his touch, which inflated his hope. Another thought struck him: *If she can't live in Fae, am I willing to live in the human realm for her?* He was sure his father wanted him to train to take his place now that Reid was gone, but he'd never seen himself being the king's right-hand man, had never felt the duty Reid did to their people. Sure, he cared about the Seelie kingdom, but his family had always come first. To him, he was only in the guard because his father and brother were.

"Penny for your thoughts." Her soft voice called to him.

He looked up into her hazel eyes and saw the soft way they studied his face, as if they could see right through him. "I was just thinking about the future."

"What do you mean?"

"I hadn't really considered the implications of Reid being gone yet. He was training to take my father's place at the king's side when the time was right, but now..."

"He's gone." Callie scooted closer.

"Right, so I'm not sure if his duty now falls onto my shoulders."

"Would you want it to?"

"No, I don't think so. I guess I'm still so young I thought I'd have time to figure out what I wanted to do. I joined the guard because it was where my dad and brother were, and I do like some aspects of it, but I never really thought... I guess I've always just done what was expected of me. I've never really thought about what *I* want before."

"Looks like some things aren't so different for Fae and humans after all. We all struggle with wanting to please our parents but also follow our own path. Close your eyes." She moved close enough for him to feel her body heat against his side, angling herself so she was facing him. "I said, close your eyes." She rolled her own at his lack of obedience and placed her hands over his eyes to ensure they were closed. "Now picture yourself in five years. What do you see?"

You. He bit back the word. The image of her laughing and holding his hand danced across his eyelids, the two of them visiting Eshna and Amina, watching Eshna grow into a teenager. "Still in the guard," he replied, which was a half-truth. He still had time left to serve the king in some capacity.

He felt her hand drift away from his face and wrap around his own. "Fifteen years?" Her tone was soft, and he wondered if she was picturing the same thing.

The image in his mind morphed into an older, more mature version of Callie picking up a little girl with curly red hair and golden eyes, swinging her into the air as the two of them laughed with such joy it made him breathless. His fingers laced between hers and tightened. He swallowed hard and caught his breath, heart pounding, each beat echoing her name in his chest. Unable to answer her, he opened his eyes.

She was studying him carefully and mistook his silence for uncertainty. Giving him a reassuring smile, she squeezed his hand. "It's okay, you still have plenty of time to figure it out."

The thing was, he had figured it out. His earlier resolve to let her go and let find her own happiness completely dissipated. He knew beyond a shadow of a doubt that the one thing he wanted most in life was her, and it didn't matter where he went or what he did for work as long as he had her by his side. His soul called to hers. Now, if only he could convince her to give him another chance.

CHAPTER 25

CALLIE STRETCHED, RUNNING her hand across the warm surface she rested upon. She blinked sleepily, noticing the sky was still dark and her warm pillow was moving up and down in sync with Evin's breathing. She froze. She was pretty sure she had fallen asleep cocooned in her own blanket on the other side of the fire, definitely not wrapped in his arms. She wondered how she'd ended up there—had she had another nightmare? She couldn't remember dreaming, but it was possible. She briefly debated moving away from his warmth but then his arm pulled her tighter against him, and she sighed, giving in to the temptation, snuggling a little deeper into his chest, his warmth thawing a bit more of her heart.

A few hours later she woke to only her blanket. She frowned, wondering if she had dreamed his warmth. Sunlight filtered in through the opening of the cave, so she knew they should probably get going. Her frown deepened as she noted Evin's absence, sighing in relief when she spotted his supplies tucked neatly beside their bag. *Stupid girl, of course he wouldn't just leave you in the middle of Fae. You know him*, she chastised herself and then groaned, feeling the familiar ache in her heart when she thought about him. *He has also lied to you before. He could do it again.* But the more she tried to convince herself to hold on to her grudge, the less conviction she felt. Every action, every word over the last few days had chipped away at her icy heart. The only thing holding her back now was her own stubbornness. *Well, that and the fact that he's not human and I am.* She shook the thought loose. It had no place here. She needed to focus on getting home before the time differential made her lose her job and only hope at paying for a college education. She carefully packed away the rest of their things as Evin reentered the cave, a small pouch full of berries and a refill of water in hand.

"That better be for me, because you do not want to see me hangry, my friend."

"Hangry?" His lips twitched at the corners.

"So hungry you get angry…hangry," she explained.

He bit his lip, but she could see the amusement clear on his face as he handed the fruit over. "Well, no one would want you to get *hangry*."

She shoved a handful of berries into her mouth, almost moaning as their sweet juice hit her tongue. Nothing in her world tasted quite like their food. She could see how those old tales about humans becoming addicted to Fae food had originated. It's hard to go back to steak from the local diner when you've tasted filet mignon. "Did you want some?" she asked with a full mouth, a tiny bit of juice dribbling down her chin before she could wipe it away with the back of her hand.

No longer hiding his amusement, Evin grinned widely.

"Thank you, but I already ate. As soon as you're done, we can go."

"Do you think I could walk for a bit? I feel like my legs need some time to stretch before climbing aboard the Evin Express." She waved her hand in his direction and his loud booming laugh echoed off the cavern walls.

"The Evin Express? Is that what we're calling it?" His amber eyes glowed.

"Well, that's what I'm calling it at least." She shrugged, tossing another handful of berries into her mouth before reaching for the water he still held. He handed it to her, and she took a few gulps, finishing off the last of the fruit.

"I don't know whether I should be flattered or insulted by your train comparison."

She smirked. "If the shoe fits." He narrowed his eyes playfully at her intentionally vague response. She took one more sip of water before handing it back to him. "All right, let's get this show on the road."

He seemingly blinked out of existence, only to return a few moments later with a full pouch of water.

"Still not used to that," she mumbled. She wasn't sure which was weirder, thinking about the fact that she had been moving at that speed for most of their travels or watching him do it. She slung the pack over her shoulder before following him out of the cave and into the sun.

They had been walking for about 30 minutes when she agreed to hop on his back. She was tempted to whistle like a train as she climbed on to keep the Evin Express joke going but thought better of it. Still, she couldn't resist whispering, "All aboard!" which she was pretty sure he heard based on the way his fingers tightened around her thighs.

They were just a few miles outside of town when he

stopped for a rest. "I'm going to scout ahead for a few minutes, check the roads before we make our way back to my place. From there, you can rest while I go find out what I can about Deryn."

"Think that's a good idea?" she asked, remembering when she had last been left alone in the woods. She could go a lifetime without coming across another goblin.

"No, but the risk is less than taking you without knowing who we may run into."

"And if someone or something comes along while you're gone?"

"I shouldn't be gone that long, ten minutes tops, and it's not like you're unarmed." He gestured toward the poisoned dagger strapped to her leg.

"Good point." She smiled, fingering the handle of her new weapon.

He hesitated before mumbling, "Screw it," and pulling her in for a hug, pressing a light kiss against her temple. Her arms wound around his waist reflexively before he released her and stepped away. With one last glance over his shoulder, he was gone.

She took a deep breath and studied her surroundings: *trees, trees, and more trees—oh, and some bushes and grass as well. Just a regular old forest,* she told herself until she heard an unfamiliar bird chirping in the distance. She sat down against a tree, knowing she should conserve her energy. She pulled her new dagger out of its sheath before she sat and traced its handle with her fingertips. She lost herself in thoughts of how they could work together to kill the quanlier, finally bringing closure to their quest and allowing her to return to a normal life.

After some time, she heard the bird call again, slightly

closer, and she whistled a response, mimicking its call. The bird repeated its unique tune, and again she returned the whistle.

"I wouldn't do that if I were you," a voice warned behind her. She jumped up, turning to face the stranger with the dagger held in front of her. A tall Fae stood in the distance. His golden hair was swept back on top of his head, appearing longer on top than on the sides, and his lightly bronzed skin seemed to glimmer as the sunlight filtered through the trees. She swallowed, holding the dagger defensively, ready to strike if need be.

"Careful there, lass, that weapon looks a little sharp. Don't want you to hurt yourself." He winked at her.

She narrowed her eyes. "It wouldn't be me I'd hurt. I'll have you know I can and will fight to defend myself against you or anyone else."

"Well, that's good seeing as the creature you've been talking to has been known to pluck out the eyes of men."

She swallowed hard. "The bird?" It hadn't even crossed her mind that it could be something other than a bird making those whistling calls.

He chuckled. "Oh, you're definitely not from around here." He took in her features, his eyes lingering on her ears and eyes. "If I had to take a guess, I would say you're a *long* way from home. I'm also pretty sure if I swept your hair back from your face, I'd discover a dainty pair of rounded ears."

Her spine stiffened in response, and she fought to maintain her poker face and fighting stance. *Shit. Where's Evin?*

"Did you get lost?" He stepped closer, and her eyes were finally able to make out his distinctly Fae features. He hadn't even bothered to glamour himself, and when her eyes found his, seeing the familiar shade of burnt orange, a brief flash of memory flickered through her mind. A blond-haired, orange-eyed Fae had helped them rescue Ianthe the previous year, one who had altered Casimir's memories.

"Wait a minute—I know you." She relaxed her stance but kept a firm grip on her dagger. Just because he had rescued her best friend one time didn't mean he was a good guy.

"Oh, you do?" He seemed amused by her but unable to recall who she was. "Seems highly unlikely since I don't often visit your world." He continued walking toward her until they were only a few feet apart.

"Ianthe," she stated, hoping it would jog his memory. His feet froze in place, and he tilted his head to the side, studying her once again but in a whole new light.

"Now, this is an interesting twist...Callie, is it?"

She nodded. "You'll have to pardon me, but I don't remember your name. It seems we were both preoccupied with other things that night."

"Maddock, one of the Seelie king's guard." He held his hand out in front of him, and she grasped it in her own, shaking it.

"It's a pleasure to meet you."

"What are you doing here? Are you in need of hel—" His last words were cut off as Evin suddenly materialized between them, shoving Callie back while holding his sword up to Maddock's chest, resting the tip against his tunic.

Maddock put both hands up, his orange eyes now glowing and a smile gracing his face, transforming it from handsome to devastating. "Evin...well, this just keeps getting even more interesting. I was just asking our friend

Callie if she needed any help." Evin growled in response, and Maddock's smile turned into a full-out grin. "I don't mean either of you any harm. As you recall, the last time you were in a sticky situation, I graciously helped all parties, including this lovely creature behind you."

Evin growled again, thrusting the sword forward just enough that it pierced Maddock's shirt and rested against his bare skin.

"Pardon my wording, Evin, but if either or both of you are in need of assistance, I can offer it to you. Now, if you would please remove your sword, I do believe you owe me a new shirt."

"And why should I?"

Maddock sighed, rolling his eyes. "Do you honestly think I have any interest in Callie beyond helping her return to her best friend, whom I would prefer to keep on my good side?" Evin stared at Maddock for another moment before pulling his sword back and sheathing it.

"You're lucky I didn't use the new one."

"If it's anything like the dagger your lady is holding, I would say I agree with you there. Does she know what a dangerous weapon she wields?"

"Excuse me! I am right here. You don't need to talk about me as if I'm not." Callie cut in, shoving her way around Evin and shaking her head, all the while knowing she relished seeing him be all protective and possessive of her. "And yes, I know exactly what weapon I have. It's laced with wolfsbane, the ideal blade for protection against a quanlier."

"The quanlier?" Maddock's eyes widened. "Is it here?"

"No, it's still in the human realm," Evin replied, not liking where the discussion was headed.

"But, then why would she need—it's tracking her, isn't it?" Maddock asked, though he could tell the answer by the hard line of Evin's lips. "That's why you're here." Maddock whistled lowly. "Do you need any assistance? I only have the day off, but I could ask the king to allow me to assist you."

"No, we'll be fine," Evin replied.

Callie elbowed him in the side and coughed. "Deryn." At least one of them was thinking straight.

He could still feel the adrenaline pumping through his veins from discovering her with another Fae. The fear of losing her was so palpable he could taste it, but she was right. It wouldn't hurt to ask Maddock if he knew anything. "Actually, on second thought, we're looking for someone, a Dyr."

Maddock whistled again. "You think a Dyr is responsible for the quanlier? Wow, that's some heavy magic right there—ancient stuff. I thought most of that bloodline had thinned out by now, but then again, up until last year, I also thought the same about Changelings."

"I'm actually a little surprised you know about them. I mean, I had heard stories before now, but…"

"I probably heard the same stories. You know how the elders like to talk, scary stories to get the youngins to fall in line, but most of the time, those stories are based on truth. My mother used to tell me about a witch in the woods who could control dangerous creatures and sic them on little boys who wandered too far from home. Sure kept me from straying too far." Maddock studied the two of them. "You're serious, though? About a Dyr being responsible? What evidence do you have?"

Callie pulled the crumpled note out of her pocket and passed it over to Maddock.

His eyebrows rose as he read its message. "And this is…"

"Alyss," Evin supplied, and Maddock drew in a sharp breath. "You may be able to help us. Being at the palace every day, you probably overhear things. Have you heard of the name Deryn before? I have from a somewhat trustworthy source in the borderlands that there was a girl named Deryn who was a Dyr who used to live by his grandfather's village. We're most likely not looking for Deryn exactly, but a family member who inherited her unique ability."

Maddock closed his eyes, whispering the name Deryn repeatedly as he racked his memory. "I know I've heard that name before…give me a few minutes."

Callie measured the silence in heartbeats. If they could find the person responsible without even entering Evin's village, it would save them so much time. Who knew how long they would have to wait—that is if they could even find the information at all. They might have to change plans and focus on killing the beast then setting a trap for any more that might show up.

Maddock paced back and forth, running his hands through his hair. After a few minutes of silence, his steps faltered and his eyes opened, glowing a brilliant orange. "Oh shit—Bronwen. It's Bronwen."

"Lady Bronwen?" Evin repeated, his words dripping with disbelief.

"Yes. After her encounter with the Changeling, I did a little digging around in her head to see if Conall's story checked out. She was pretty messed up over the whole thing and willing to let me in if I removed her memory of sleeping with the stranger she thought was Conall. As I was sifting through her thoughts and memories to pinpoint the moment, I came across one of her with her grandmother.

I'm pretty sure her father called her grandmother Deryn."
He closed his eyes again. "Must be her mother's side, as
there's definitely no resemblance to her father there."

"But why would she…" Evin's voice trailed off, his
eyes going wide.

"Conall!" both men exclaimed at the same time.

"This is bad," Evin mumbled before directing his conversation toward Maddock entirely. Both men spoke so
quickly, discussing things and people Callie didn't know
until she felt almost dizzy she was so lost.

"Ahem!" She cleared her throat loudly. "A little explanation would be wise here, especially after declaring this
has something to do with my bestie's lover boy."

Both men turned their eyes toward her, and Evin's
cheeks flushed pink. "Sorry. Um, I guess the best way to
word this is that Bronwen and Conall were kind of a thing,
or at least spent a night or two together before he met
Ianthe. She didn't exactly take his rejection well this last
time, and mix in the fact that Casimir apparently pretended
to be Conall and spent some one-on-one time with her…"

Callie's memory jogged loose, recalling stories Ianthe
had told her about what happened when she left the Seelie palace. Her breath quickened, struck with realization.
"Beware the lover scorned," she whispered. "Alyss's pre-
diction is right—it just wasn't either of our lovers. That
means the quanlier was sent for him or Ianthe." Callie's
heart thudded. "Evin! We have to go back," she yelled.
"We can't let them face it alone. We have to protect her!"

She didn't realize she was shaking until Evin pulled
her into his arms. "Shh, *mo rua*. She'll be okay." He
rubbed his hands up and down her back soothingly. "She
has Conall to protect her, and he is a fierce warrior. He
won't let anything happen to her, but you're right—we do

need to get back to them and let them know what's going on." He brought his hands up to cup her face and sighed, staring down into her eyes, amber shifting to brilliant gold. She lost herself in his gaze for a moment, in the pure emotion it conveyed. "You know the instant we cross back into your realm, the quanlier will be tracking you."

Maddock coughed, drawing their attention to him once more. "I could watch her while you—"

"NO!" Callie yelled, surprising all three of them. "I am not going to sit here twiddling my thumbs while the three people I care about most outside of my family are in danger. I'm going with you." Her hazel eyes were wild, a fierceness Evin hadn't seen before blazing within them. He was in the middle of wondering if he was included in the three people she had mentioned when she added, "Besides, you can use me as bait."

"No way. Not happening," he insisted.

Maddock clucked his tongue. "You have to admit, having her with you would bring the creature right to your front door." Evin scowled at Maddock until he backed up, throwing his hands out in a placating gesture. "Just a suggestion, man. If you and Conall are ready, the two of you could easily defeat it. I can stay here and track Bronwen. I'll let the king know who is behind the attack and see how he would like to proceed."

"Thank you, Maddock. That would be a great help. If we can remove her from the equation, at least then she won't be able send any more creatures."

"I'll be in contact." Maddock nodded. "Callie, it was wonderful to see you again." He winked at her, earning another low growl from Evin. Maddock sniggered as he hiked off into the distance.

"So, I guess that means we're not going into town,"

Callie surmised.

Evin sighed. "I suppose not. We should get to Conall and Ianthe as quickly as possible."

"And what happens when we leave Fae?" She bit her lip nervously, uncomfortable with the thought of a deadly creature being able to track her.

"We hope it's daylight and move as quickly as possible. Quanliers are nocturnal, so it won't come hunting until night, and hopefully by then we'll have a plan worked out."

Callie nodded, taking a deep breath. "Okay, let's do this." She motioned for Evin to turn so she could hop on his back. Despite her nervousness, she couldn't resist releasing a train whistle sound as she climbed up and wrapped her legs around him. He shook his head but couldn't hide the slight lift in the corners of his mouth. She smiled, hoping to drown her nerves in the sensation of his warmth. *Evin will protect me. He'll kill the quanlier and no one else will get hurt. It has to work. Please God, let it work.* She repeated the positive thoughts in her head as she closed her eyes and wished for the best.

CHAPTER 26

"**PLEASE BE HOME,**" Callie whispered as she climbed off Evin's back and stepped onto her best friend's driveway. They'd lucked out; based on the position of the sun, it had been about noon when they'd arrived back in the human realm, and with Evin's ability, it had taken little time for them to travel into town and arrive at Ianthe's house. She approached the door cautiously, Evin's hand resting on the small of her back, his eyes taking in every detail of the neighborhood. She raised her fist to knock but it was flung open and she was practically tackled to the ground.

"You're here! You're safe! I've been so worried, Cal." Ianthe's words blurred together as Callie's sides ached.

"Um, Thee, maybe a little less squeezing would help. I can't really breathe."

"Oh! Of course." Ianthe released her, stepping back.

"Maybe we should continue this conversation inside, love." Conall spoke from over her shoulder. "Away from prying eyes." He motioned toward their clothing, and Callie remembered they were still dressed for the Fae realm and might attract a few wandering gazes.

"I guess it is a little late in the year for a Ren fair," Callie joked.

Ianthe laughed before explaining what the renaissance festival was to Conall as they walked inside.

"Is your dad home?" Callie asked.

"No, he's at work, but he's been worried about you too. We had to fill him in so he could lie to your parents about being with us. I've mostly been hiding at home so I wouldn't be seen by your mom or grandma. They think we're on vacation and stole you along with us. In fact, I have some of your clothes up in my room that I took from your house as part of our cover story."

"My car?" Callie asked, remembering the night she abandoned it on the side of the road.

"My dad had it towed to a repair shop and all fixed up for you. I think it still needs to be picked up though. He was at least smart enough to grab your purse and phone from the car. I was going to lecture you when you got back, but then I saw your phone was dead, and I know if you had been able to, you would have called me instead of walking around like a dumbass while a creature with a taste for human innards wandered the streets."

Callie blushed and stared at her feet. She had known at the time it wasn't a smart move, but what choice had she really had? Would she have been any safer in her car just sitting there? "I did try to call you, but I didn't want to wait until morning when someone might find me in my car, and the party wasn't that far away."

Ianthe waved her hand dismissively. "Water under the

bridge. The most important thing is that you're here and you're safe." She pulled her into another hug, this one not quite as tight.

"Have there been any other deaths?" Evin directed his question toward Conall.

"Only one, and it took a week or so before it attacked again, although I'm not sure why."

"We do." Callie blushed again. "It, um, has the scent of my blood, so we think it was probably tracking me. I had hoped no one else would have to die."

"If it has your scent then—" Conall inhaled sharply.

"It will start tracking me the moment it wakes," Callie interrupted, and Ianthe gasped.

"There's more," Evin added. "We know why it's here. Seems we have a Dyr in the Seelie court, someone we're both familiar with and who may have reasons to send the beast here."

"A Dyr?" Ianthe asked at the same time Conall asked, "Who?"

"Rare Fae that can control evil animals and get them to do their bidding," Callie explained. She narrowed her eyes briefly on Conall. "And you can't think of any Seelie who might have a reason to send a creature here, perhaps an ex of yours?" She raised her eyebrows.

"No…wait…*Bronwen?*"

"Ding ding ding! We have a winner," Callie jeered.

Ianthe frowned. "I thought you explained that it wasn't you she was with the last time in the garden."

"I did! I swear!"

"Then why would she send a creature over here?"

"Probably 'cause she's cray." Both boys shot Callie a

look. "What?! I haven't met the girl, but most mentally stable women would move on after being dumped, not send a killer creature over to where her ex's new girl lives. I'm just saying she probably has a loose screw or two."

"Maddock is tracking Bronwen now. He's going to inform King Lachlan that she is the one responsible for the quanlier and see how he would like to proceed. In the meantime, we need to come up with a plan for how to kill it, because the minute the sun sets, it will be on its way to wherever Callie is."

"Which reminds me—if I'm going to act as bait tonight, I'd like to at least pop in on my family…you know, in case things go wrong." It took a lot to admit this part. Even knowing she had volunteered to serve as bait, she was afraid. There were so many things that could go badly. She knew the risk and was willing to take it, but before she did, she wanted to see her family one more time, wanted to let them know she was safe, just in case.

"Don't even say that!" Ianthe turned her attention to the boys. "We can't use her as bait. I won't allow it. Find another way." She crossed both arms over her chest.

Conall stepped closer, placing a hand on her shoulder. "Love, the quanlier will track her no matter what. At least if we use her as bait, we can control the circumstances and location where the beast will show up. It gives us better odds of being able to defeat it."

"It's okay, Thee. I'm not entirely defenseless either. I have a new toy, see." Callie slid her skirt up to show where the dagger was strapped above her knee. "It's spiked, too, laced with poison made special for our little beastie."

"That still doesn't make me okay with this. And I suppose you want me to stay at home while all of this is going down?" Ianthe took one look at Conall and knew she'd guessed correctly. "Well, mister, that's not happening. I'm not staying at home. If my bestie is going to be used as bait, you better believe I'm going to be right there fighting alongside her. I don't care what you say, don't care if it goes against your instincts as my guard or your orders from my father. I'm going."

Evin wisely chose not to voice his concerns at that moment. In all honesty, another set of eyes would be helpful, and if Conall had been training her to fight, all the better. Besides, he recognized the same defiance he'd seen earlier in Callie's eyes and knew better than to argue with it.

Conall, on the other hand, apparently hadn't learned yet. He had just opened his mouth to speak when Ianthe shot him a withering look. He snapped his jaw shut and swallowed whatever he had been about to say.

"Okay, now that that's settled, let's get you changed. Conall, can you take Evin to your place and get him something a little more appropriate to wear while Cal and I catch up?" Ianthe took Callie by the elbow, practically dragging her up to her room, not even bothering to wait for a reply from Conall. "'Kay, thanks. Love you, bye!" she called over her shoulder.

Callie glanced back at Evin and saw him studying her. When she smiled reassuringly at him, he took that to mean she was in good hands.

"They'll be fine. I promise. There's no safer place here than Ianthe's house, and we'll only be a few minutes," Conall assured him before he was able to tear his gaze away from the now empty stairwell.

"Do you really think I need a change of clothes?" he asked as they walked outside and down the street to Conall's house.

"Your leather pants should be fine, but a different shirt

would probably help draw less attention, especially if you plan on accompanying Callie to see her family, as I'm sure you do."

Evin nodded. "Of course. Any ideas for how or where to best attack the quanlier?"

"I'll talk it over with Ianthe since she knows the neighborhood, but I do know there is a dog park close by. It's gated and fairly open, which may help us. I'll check with her and see if she has any better ideas. I have to be honest with you—if she's with us, my attention will be split. I'll help you as best I can, but my number one priority will be to keep her safe."

"I wouldn't expect anything less."

"So, spill the tea!" Ianthe practically demanded the moment they reached her room.

"I don't have anything to spill."

"Oh, puh-lease, like I'm going to believe that. I know you too well, so start talking, missy." Ianthe pulled out a duffle bag from her closet and thrust it in Callie's direction before sitting on her bed and staring up expectantly.

Callie sighed, rummaging through the bag to find what she wanted to wear. "Fine. He rescued me the night my car died. My stupid flip-flop broke, causing me to trip and cut my foot, which is how the quanlier has my scent. Evin caught me and whisked me away to Fae. We traveled to the borderlands to find weapons and get information. I got kidnapped by goblins and was auctioned off in a slave market, we rescued a Djinn girl and returned her home, and at some point I think I fell in love with him."

"You're in love with him?"

"Seriously? I just told you about being kidnapped by goblins and sold on the slave market and that's the part you focus on?" She pulled out a pair of shorts before remembering the dagger and how it might be hard to conceal. She tossed the shorts aside.

"Of course I'm curious about the rest, but you obviously survived it, so now I'm focusing on the most pressing matter—the fact that you just admitted to me, and probably to yourself for the first time, that you may be in love with him."

Callie sighed. "Do you have a skirt I can wear?"

"A skirt? Really? Also, I'm not accepting this as a change in conversation."

"Yes, a skirt. I need something that will hide the dagger. I can strap it on higher, but I will need something over it."

Ianthe got up, rummaging through her drawers before flinging a pair of cotton shorts toward Callie. She then proceeded to her closet where she selected a hi-lo flowy gray skirt. "This work?"

"Perfect. Better than just the skirt, too—wouldn't want to worry about flashing my undies while we're trying to slay an otherworldly creature." Callie unstrapped the dagger and slipped her dress over her head before pulling on the shorts and then stepping into the skirt. The shorter part of the skirt hit right at her knees. When she shifted the dagger up to her thigh, the skirt hid it perfectly, and the shorts gave her the range of movement she'd need to fight. Luckily, it also worked well with the boots she was already wearing.

"So, when do you think you started falling for him?"

As promised, Ianthe redirected the conversation back to the topic at hand.

"It's hard to pinpoint exactly when. I can't tell if it happened so slowly or quickly that I missed the exact moment, if there was one, or maybe it was all the little ones that added up." She shook her head. "Is love supposed to be like that? Like you can't tell when you started loving the person, and now you just know how much it would suck to be without them?" She searched through her bag some more before pulling out a white tank top and slipping it over her head.

"It's difficult to say. I think falling in love is different for everyone. I was definitely attracted to Conall at first, but it took a while before I could say I loved him. It wasn't until we realized how dire our circumstances were that I could admit how strong my feelings were. I also think being in incredibly dangerous situations can escalate feelings and cause them to develop more quickly."

"I've been fighting my attraction to him for some time. I know he wants me to forgive him, but I still don't know how this will work. He's Fae and I'm human." She sat on the bed and leaned her shoulder against Ianthe's.

"Listen, it's not like you have to figure things out right now, and who's to say it would be forever? It's not that I'm discrediting your feelings in any way, but most relationships at our age aren't lasting ones. We're young. We have time to figure it out. You have time. If you want to give it a shot, you can, and it may last, or it might not."

"Oh, Thee, when did you get so wise?"

Ianthe snorted. "Besides, since I've had your phone, I also know of a certain other cutie who's been texting you, and I may or may not have replied on your behalf."

Callie leaned back. "You what?!"

"Don't worry, I made sure any flirting was kept strictly PG...well, maybe a little PG-13." Ianthe smiled.

"Thee! I can't believe you."

"I kid, I kid. Strictly friendly replies, I swear. I just didn't want Jordan to think you were ignoring him and move on if you wanted to start dating him. I was just looking out for you."

"Thanks."

"Although, you do realize you will have to let him down at some point now that you know how you feel, right?"

"I know."

"Does Evin know?"

"No, so don't say anything. Pinky swear?" She held her pinky out, and Ianthe looped hers around it in return.

"My lips are sealed. Now, let's see if the boys are back and make a game plan for how we're going to slay the mighty beast and save the kingdom!" Her voice took on an announcer-like quality as if she were a narrator from a fantasy anime.

CHAPTER 27

"**YOU DIDN'T HAVE** to come with me," Callie replied, looking Evin over once again. Something about the leather pants and snug white t-shirt did something for her. He looked good enough to eat. Judging by the way his gaze kept flicking toward her legs, he'd probably have said the same thing about her.

"And miss the chance to finally meet your family? Not a chance."

His eyes shimmered, glowing slightly when they finally left her legs and met her gaze. She snapped her fingers. She'd gotten so used to seeing him without his glamour, but now he would definitely need it. "Glamour, Evin! Did you forget where you are?"

"Oh yeah. I guess I'd just gotten used to being myself around you." He smiled, his features blurring slightly right before her eyes, his ears rounding, his nose and jawline becoming less distinct. Finally, the tips of his teeth smoothed out. His caramel-colored skin still had a slight glow to it, but his eyes did not. Seeing him look like a human again actually made her miss his distinctly Fae features. She frowned.

"Why the sour face? Do I not look presentable?" He looked himself over from top to bottom. Thankfully he'd left his sword in Ianthe's car, which they had borrowed. How was she going to explain his presence? She was supposed to have been gone with Ianthe on vacation. Before she could give it any further thought, Sean plowed out the door and straight into her, wrapping his arms around her waist.

"You're home! How was your trip? Where did you guys go? Was it Harry Potter World? Did you have a good time?" He bombarded her with questions, one after another. "Wait—who's he?"

"My trip was great, thank you. Yes, we went to Harry Potter World, and it was everything I'd dreamed it would be. He's...um..." She turned and looked over her shoulder. "He's Evin...Conall's cousin." It was the only thing that came to mind that might make sense.

"Conall's cousin? Did he go with you or is he visiting now?"

She ruffled the top of Sean's hair. *Man, I missed him.* "Both. Did you grow while I was gone? You seem taller. I told you—you aren't allowed to grow any more." She hoped the topic change would keep him from questioning Evin's presence further.

Sean giggled. "That's not how it works, sissy. I'm going to be taller than you one day, just you wait."

"I'm sure you are, kid, but you've still got a few years before you hit puberty. Is Grams home?"

"Yep. Mom's about to leave for work, though, so you should let her know you're back." He took Callie's hand

and pulled her in behind him.

"You can wait out here if you want," she threw over her shoulder at Evin.

"And miss meeting your family? I wouldn't dream of it," he replied.

When they made it inside, her mom was throwing things into her lunch bag. "Oh, Callie, you're back already. Joel wasn't sure when you guys would make it back, something about possible detours along the way or extending the trip to visit his family. I can't quite remember, but I knew you were in good hands." She reached over to her daughter and hugged her before noticing Evin trailing behind them. "Oh, hello, and who might you be?"

"My name is Evin. Pleased to meet you, ma'am." He held his hand out for her to shake.

"Marilyn," she replied, shaking his hand in return.

"He's Conall's cousin," Sean piped in, shoving an apple into his mouth and taking a loud, crunchy bite.

"Oh. I didn't know you were going with them." Her mom seemed flustered for a moment.

"They picked me up on the way back—one of those detours you mentioned." He grinned, and Callie was only slightly surprised he was able to lie so convincingly.

"Oh, yes. Will you be staying for a while?" her mother asked.

He reflexively looked to Callie for an answer and she winced, hoping her mother didn't see his glance, but she did. "I'm not sure, ma'am. I don't really have any set plans at the moment."

Her mother grinned. "I'm sure you'll figure it out." She shot a wink at her daughter that had Callie's cheeks turning pink. "Okay, kids, I better go before I'm late. Be good for Grams." Marilyn hugged and kissed her two children before making her way to the door. "Nice to meet you, Evin. Hope to see you around."

Callie groaned. "Love you, Mom!" she added before the door closed. It would suck if the last thing her mother remembered about her was that she groaned at her matchmaker attempt. "Where's Grams?" she asked Sean, knowing there was one more person she needed to see.

"I think she's in her room," Sean said with his mouth full. Callie turned toward the hallway, unsure if she wanted Evin to follow her. She headed down the hall, noticing that Evin hung back in the kitchen with her brother. "Grams?"

"Oh, Callie-kins, is that you?" Her grandmother emerged from Sean's room. "I was just putting away some laundry. How was your trip? I didn't know you'd be back today." She pulled Callie in and hugged her fiercely, same as always. Callie hugged her back, taking a moment to breathe her in.

Callie smiled. "It was great. We didn't know either."

"So, will you be joining us for dinner?"

"Actually—" Callie was cut off by a loud booming laugh from the kitchen, one too low-pitched to belong to her brother. Her belly flipped.

"Oh, do we have another guest?" Her grandmother practically shoved her out of the way. When they reached the kitchen, she elbowed Callie in the stomach. "Who do we have here?"

"Ow, Grams, geez. That's Evin, Conall's cousin who's in town. We picked him up for a visit on our way back."

"Well aren't you just a handsome young thing?" her grandmother purred.

"Grams!"

"Well, he is. You can at least admit that. You'd have to be blind not to see it."

"And here I thought Mom was bad. Apparently she learned it from you."

Evin chuckled. "Pleasure to meet you, ma'am."

"Pfft. None of this *ma'am* business. It's Grams. That's what all of Callie's friends call me." She stuck out her hand and shook his, practically giggling like a schoolgirl.

"Okay! And that's our cue to go," Callie announced. She didn't want to see her grandmother drool over Evin anymore. It was pretty disturbing.

"Leaving so soon? Why don't you both join us for dinner?" She still held Evin's hand, shaking it dumbly. Callie shook her head. Her grandma had never acted this way around Conall.

"Wish we could, but Uncle Joel is expecting us," Evin lied.

"Well, come back and see us again soon." She finally extracted her hand from his. "And you, young lady—I'd ask if you're staying at Ianthe's tonight, but I'm pretty sure the answer is right in front of me." She nodded her head toward Evin.

"Grams!" Callie admonished, her cheeks burning.

"Love you, Callie-kins. You are expected home at some point tomorrow. Call if it will be after dinner."

"I will, Grams. Love you too." Callie gave her one more hug. "See you tomorrow, squirt!" she called to Sean, who had already left the kitchen and seated himself in front of the TV, game controller in hand.

"Bye, sissy! Bye, Evin! You'll have to come play with

me sometime."

Evin smiled. "I'd like that."

Grams sighed and practically swooned, and Callie couldn't fault her seeing as her heart was currently drumming against her chest.

When they got in the car, Callie turned on Evin. "Did you really have to flirt with my grandmother? I'm surprised she didn't have a heart attack."

Evin put his hand on his chest. "I did no such thing. I can't help it if the ladies in your family seem attracted to me."

Callie coughed, choking on her own saliva a bit.

Evin laughed, enjoying her discomfort for a moment then turning his voice soft. "I liked meeting them. Thank you for letting me."

The sincerity in his eyes shot right into her heart. She wasn't sure how to respond, so she started the car and drove them back to Ianthe's house.

Night came faster than any of them would've liked. They ate what they could at Ianthe's for dinner and came up with a plan to lure the quanlier out, ultimately deciding the dog park seemed like the best idea, especially since it was closed at night and less likely to involve any innocent bystanders. Joel hadn't been happy with the plan in the least bit and insisted on going with them. It was quite the argument and he tried to assert his point, but eventually he conceded to sitting in his car with one hand on his phone in case they needed emergency assistance. He drove them to the park, hoping the beast wouldn't sense Callie while she was in the vehicle.

The air was tense and full of silence, as if everyone was holding their breath. Evin thought back to his discussion with Callie's little brother in the kitchen. Sean had been a rather curious ten-year-old, asking all sorts of questions, including if he was Callie's boyfriend. He'd answered as honestly as he could, telling him only if Callie wanted him to be. When Sean had followed that one up by asking if he'd ever kissed Callie, he had been too stunned to answer. Sean had taken his silence as a yes, and the look on the boy's face had made him almost double over in laughter. He was thankful Callie and her grandmother hadn't joined them until after that moment. He reached over and squeezed her hand. He had promised he wouldn't let anything happen to her, and he was damn well going to make sure he kept that promise.

When the SUV stopped in the parking lot, they were a bundle of nerves. "You girls have your phones. Call me if you need me. Gentlemen, know that the only reason I'm staying here is because my daughter has begged me to, but so help me, if anything happens to either of those girls, I will kill or at the very least maim each of you."

Callie almost laughed at the slight panic on each of their faces. It was humorous to think of a human being able to do them any damage, but she also knew if it came down to it, neither of them would fight back.

"Is everyone armed?" Joel asked, and they each chimed in with a yes, or yep in Ianthe's case. Apparently, since the quanlier had appeared, Conall had upped her combat training to include weapons, and she had quite the knack for throwing knives.

Callie fingered the handle of her dagger through her skirt while Conall spoke. "Remember, no close contact.

Ianthe, throw to slow. Our weapons will only do so much without wolfsbane. It'll be up to Evin to deliver the killing blow. Callie, once the beast shows itself, you will need to hide. Either get back to the car or try for the public restrooms."

"Sir, yes sir!" Callie mock saluted, needing some humor to break the tension.

"All right. Evin, get Callie into position. Ianthe, I need a moment," Conall added, stepping out of the vehicle.

"Be safe! I'm serious about the maiming, and it will start with your most valuable part," Joel called out, making Callie smile. She loved having a surrogate dad to look out for her.

Callie climbed out after Evin and watched as Conall approached Ianthe, pulling her into his arms and pressing his forehead against hers. She looked away, allowing them a moment of privacy. Evin tugged lightly on her left arm, reminding her that at some point during the ride he had grabbed her hand and still hadn't let go. The gate clanged behind them as they entered the fenced park. They found a picnic table next to a tree surrounded by open grass, the perfect place for Callie to sit and be able to scramble up the tree or back toward the bathrooms if necessary.

She wrapped her arms around him, taking Evin by surprise. He smoothed his hand down her hair. "*Is tú mo ghrá. I won't let anything happen to you, mo rua.*" His voice was low and gravelly, causing her to clutch him tighter. She wasn't sure what he'd said, but she knew it was important.

"Now would be a great time to tell me whatever you just said in English, please."

He chuckled. "After." Pulling back, he stared into her hazel eyes. At some point he had dropped his glamour, allowing her to see him for all he was. His eyes were like molten gold, and she melted into him, pressing her lips against his. The kiss started soft and sweet but quickly flared with passion and slight desperation, as if they couldn't get enough of each other or the moment. He reluctantly pulled away with a sigh and cupped her face. "I expect more of that when we finish."

She blushed as he rubbed his thumb across the pink stain and smiled, pressing one more kiss to her lips before vanishing and reappearing a few yards away. She sighed and sat on the table, her legs wobbly. Even with the darkening sky, she could see the smile and eyebrow raise from Ianthe, who was perched in a tree, knives in hand. Callie ran her tongue across her lips, savoring the taste of him for a moment longer until an eerily familiar shriek echoed in the distance. Her spine stiffened as she remembered why they were there and pulled her head from the clouds.

Her friends took their own battle stances as she stood on top of the table, dagger at the ready. They waited with bated breath until another haunting scream filled the air, closer this time. Callie saw Ianthe whip out her phone, probably shooting off a text to her dad before sliding it back into her pocket and picking up her daggers, at the ready.

The hair on the back of her neck stood up as she heard a low growl from behind her. She spun, staring at the large creature just on the other side of the chain link fence. Its yellow wolf-like eyes stared her down as it snarled, showing off jaggedly sharp teeth. "Uh, guys!" she yelled. She'd never seen anything like it. Even renderings of werewolves she'd seen on TV and in the movies didn't do the quanlier justice. It was larger than any wolf she'd ever seen, and while its head and limbs were wolf-like, its torso was definitely that of a muscular, hairy man. She shuddered as it ran into the fence, bouncing back with a rattling clang. It growled again and circled back. She hoped it was heading for the entrance because that was what they had planned, but they had underestimated its abilities and strength.

The quanlier came flying at the fence faster than Callie thought possible, hooking its claws into the links before beginning to ascend. It scaled the fence quickly, only slipping once before quickly regaining its footing.

"Oh shit! Evin!" she screamed. Jumping off the table, she ran in the opposite direction. When it got to the top of the fence, a sliver dagger flew through the air and pierced its shoulder. It shrieked through its long snout, teeth gleaming with saliva in the moonlight, but it kept going, launching into a flying leap from the top of the fence. Callie ran, but the quanlier was faster. It was closing in on her when Evin flashed behind her, sword at the ready, placing him directly between her and the beast. The creature paused, staring down the obstacle in the way of him pursuing his prey. Another dagger flew by, but this time, the creature dodged it. Callie heard Ianthe curse in the distance and Conall's footfalls coming closer. She glanced over her shoulder at Evin as he faced down the monster from her nightmares, her steps faltering for a moment.

"Get to the bathrooms!" he ordered, and she obeyed, veering off to the right.

The beast leaped, jumping higher than they'd all thought possible, and Evin moved quickly, trying to catch it with his sword in midair. He scraped the beast's belly, but not enough to gut him. The quanlier shrieked again, twisting and tumbling when it hit the ground but quickly recovering and continuing the chase. It seemed they were only succeeding in making it more enraged. Callie kept running, her lungs sucking in air, the bathrooms only a few yards away.

"I can't throw any more knives. They may hit Callie," Ianthe called out.

"I'm on it," Conall replied, sprinting in Callie's direction, hoping to head off the quanlier.

Evin spun around in the direction of the beast only a moment too late. It leapt again, this time catching Callie in the leg with its razor-sharp claws.

She screamed as she fell, holding the dagger flat in her hand. The wound burned fiercely, and she felt the wet drip of blood running down her leg. She pulled herself up as best she could before Conall hoisted her up, pushing her back toward the bathrooms. She stumbled, nowhere near able to run now. Conall thrust his own sword toward the creature, but it swiped him with its massive paw, knocking him away.

"Nooo!" Ianthe screamed, moving to climb back down the tree and run to help.

Struck by her bestie's scream, Callie turned to see Conall smack his back against a tree. Thankfully he recovered quickly, rolling onto his knees. "So help me, Ianthe, you better not think of coming down from that tree," he growled as he got back on his feet.

Evin used Conall's distraction to jump forward, attempting to land a shot from behind at the same time the beast leapt at Callie again, knocking her down on her back. Its teeth ripped into her left shoulder, and she screamed. She fought against the pain, thankful she hadn't dropped the dagger in her fall, and thrust it up toward the quanlier's chest until it found purchase. She hoped she nailed the bastard in the heart, or at the very least punctured a lung. Warm liquid oozed down the dagger and over her hand, and she heard the wet sound of Evin's sword as he removed it from the quanlier's back. Its lifeless body collapsed on top of her, knocking the breath from her body and pinning her arm between herself and the beast. Within an instant Evin and Conall were shoving the body off of her. She heard Ianthe scrambling down from the tree, screaming at the boys and asking if her friend was okay. Callie opened her mouth to speak but coughed wetly instead. Blood trickled out of the corner of her lips.

Conall's eyes widened as he spun to catch Ianthe, not letting her get any closer. Callie heard Ianthe beat against his chest, yelling at him to let her go.

"*Mo rua*, you must hold on. Keep fighting." She blinked at Evin as he spoke, leaning over her. He pulled his shirt over his head and balled it up, pressing it against her shoulder.

Ianthe broke free, running up to Callie's side and taking her hand. "Why isn't her blood clotting?" she asked, tears streaming down her face. "Hold on, Cal. Stay with us. You're not allowed to leave me."

Conall rested his hand against Ianthe's back. "It's the venom in the quanlier's teeth. It keeps the blood flowing."

Evin's hand trembled against her shoulder.

Conall bent down. "Here, let me."

Reluctantly, Evin allowed Conall to take his place, putting pressure on the wound. He couldn't bear to see her like that. His heart beat for her, and it had stopped the moment she'd fallen beneath the beast. He didn't know what to do, but he couldn't just sit there and watch her die. He knelt beside her. She reached for him, her fingers grazing his thigh and the coin he had in his pocket.

The coin! He pulled it out and rubbed it between his fingers. "Amina, please!" he whispered, closing his eyes and pressing a kiss against Callie's temple. The coin glowed, sizzling hot in his fingers for a second before crumbling into dust.

A breeze ruffled the trees, and the Djinn appeared before him on the other side of Callie, behind Ianthe. "Oh no, no, no, no." She shook her head back and forth, assessing the situation before cutting her gaze toward him. "Quickly, Evin, tell me what it is you wish." Her eyes watered as she stared down at the pair of them. Conall pulled Ianthe out of the way, and they heard the faint wail of sirens as Joel yelled for his daughter in the distance.

"She can't die—she can't. I wish for Callie to live. Heal her."

Callie stared helplessly at the woman, wishing to take away the pain in Evin's voice. She wanted to tell him she would be okay, that dying wasn't that terrifying as long as he stayed by her side. Her breaths were coming shorter and she knew it wouldn't be long until death claimed her, but she wasn't sure what Amina could do. She attempted to speak again but only coughed more blood. She closed her eyes against the searing pain in her shoulder and leg, their voices seeming fainter, as if she were underwater.

The Djinn studied Evin for a moment before placing a hand directly over Callie's heart. "She's lost too much blood. I'm afraid the only thing I could do now would be to stop the bleeding, but I don't think that would be enough. Her life force is fading, and Djinn wishes have their limits. However, if I have an anchor to which to tie her life force, it is possible I could save her. It's old magic and hardly ever used because it's a great risk to you both. It would require your blood and would mean sacrificing part of your life for hers. You two would be eternally bound, your life forces tied together, shared, if you will. For you, it will mean a shorter life span. For her, it will be an extension, but if death were to befall either of you, the other would follow almost instantly."

Evin stared down at his love. He couldn't lose her, not now. Ianthe sobbed in the background, and his own tears threatened to overtake him, but he shoved them away. "I'll do it."

"I must warn you, it may not work. She's lost a lot of blood, and it may be too late. If she can't fight her way out of the darkness, she'll pull you down with her and you both will perish tonight."

"If it means a chance for her to live, it's worth it," he growled, clutching Callie's hand. Her fingers no longer curled against his, and his stomach dropped. He pressed his lips against hers, faintly feeling her breath. "*Is tú mo ghrá.*"

Amina began speaking in an ancient language he wasn't familiar with, one of the Fae but particular to the Djinn. He'd only heard stories of their magic and the mysterious ways in which it worked. She grabbed his free hand and pulled a dagger from her belt, slicing his palm open. She moved his shirt from Callie's shoulder and thrust his bleeding hand on top of her wounds, holding it there while she spoke. Her words were a kind of music all their own with cadence and pauses, some spoken so softly, others a guttural yell. It was almost hypnotizing.

He felt his hand grow warm and saw brilliant white light glowing around Amina's hand, soaking into Callie's shoulder. He grew dizzy, and if he hadn't already been kneeling, he was sure his knees would have buckled. Tingles shot from his palm up his arm as if the limb had fallen asleep or the warmth was leaving his body. The light grew brighter as Amina's voice grew louder. Finally, when the tingles turned into needle-like pain, she released his hand. He lurched back, swaying as Conall caught him from behind. His vision blurred, stars swimming in his eyes.

"The bleeding stopped!" Ianthe yelled as the sirens that were in the distance now blared close by.

"I must go before the humans arrive. Watch them both closely—we're still not out of the woods," Amina instructed them. "Shall I do something with the quanlier?"

"Please," Conall replied, knowing they needed to get rid of the body so the humans wouldn't see it. She waved her hand and the beast's body transformed into that of a rabid wolf.

Ianthe pressed the shirt back against Callie's wounds as she heard Joel pointing the paramedics in their direction. Conall moved away from Evin to gather their weapons and hide them in the bushes, out of view, leaving only one of Ianthe's modern throwing knives, the one imbedded in the wolf's shoulder to explain how the animal died. With the loss of his friend's support, Evin tipped over to the side, and his stomach rolled. He fought to make his limbs move him back toward Callie, barely able to crawl the short distance. Her eyes still had not opened and he feared the worst. "No matter what, you are worth it," he whispered, his fingers snaking around hers. This time there was a faint twitch, as if her fingers were trying to clasp his. He smiled as everything went black.

CHAPTER 28

THE BEEPING SOUND of a machine in the distance gnawed at her, invading her dream. She had been sleeping, curled against Evin in the cave when the beeping first started. She knew it didn't belong there, didn't make sense; they didn't have alarms in Fae. The beeping echoed through her skull and she felt herself floating away. Slowly she opened her eyes, staring at white-pocked ceiling tiles.

"She's awake!" Grams said from somewhere in the room, and then she was peering over her. "You gave us quite the scare, Callie-kins."

Callie tried to talk but felt something blocking her. She reached up to remove it.

"Stop that," Grams scolded gently. "You'll have to wait for a nurse to do it."

It was then she realized she had a breathing tube in. She nodded slightly, frustrated she couldn't ask the million questions running through her head, like, *What the hell happened?* and *Where is Evin? Ianthe? Did they manage to kill the beast?*

"Do you remember what happened?" Grams asked, stroking Callie's hand. She shrugged her shoulders slightly. "You were attacked by that rabid wolf that's been running around town. Thank God Evin was with you." Callie's eyes widened at his name, hoping to convey what she desperately wanted to know. "He's okay, a little bruised and cut up but okay. Had to get some stitches in his hand. Seems the knife slipped and cut his palm open when he stabbed the wolf trying to protect you."

If she could have sighed, she would have. Thankfully her mother and a nurse appeared to remove the tube, though that was an experience she never wished to repeat. After a few sips of water, her throat no longer felt like it was on fire. She noted a bandage on her left shoulder and another around her calf. "Can you...can I...?" She coughed.

"Whatever it is, sweetheart, we'll get it for you. Just say the word," her mom said, placing a hand on her uninjured shoulder.

"Evin," she finally managed to get out.

Her mother smiled. "Of course. I think your grandmother already went to let them know you were awake. They've all been waiting for you since Evin was released."

"How long?" she croaked.

"Almost a full day. You gave us quite the scare. I think I aged ten years waiting for you to wake up." She knew her mother's light teasing was hiding her true fear, and Callie could only imagine how terrified she had been upon receiving the call and rushing to the ER.

A knock sounded at the door before Ianthe burst through. "Cal! You're okay! I mean I knew you would be okay, but still."

"I'll leave you to it. You guys have 15 minutes, that's it." When Ianthe opened her mouth to protest, Marilyn stopped her. "They've already bent enough rules letting me sneak you guys in. It should be immediate family only, so you will do as I say, young lady."

A sheepish "Yes ma'am" was Ianthe's only reply before she draped her arm across Callie's stomach to partially hug her and avoid her shoulder. "We were so worried about both of you after what happened."

"Both of us?" Callie's memory of what had happened after she buried her dagger into the quanlier's chest was a little hazy, but she didn't think Evin had been attacked too.

Conall coughed. "Maybe we should let Evin explain, love." He gently tugged Ianthe back. "I knew you were a fighter." He winked at her before pulling her from the room.

"But I wasn't..." She heard her best friend's voice protest as the door closed, leaving her alone with Evin.

"How are you feeling?" he asked shyly.

"Like I got bit by a savage animal." She tried to joke, but he frowned, stepping closer to her.

He picked up her hand, pressing his lips into her palm. "I thought I'd lost you."

"I thought you did too. What happened?"

He licked his lips, a nervous tick she had noticed a while ago. "Amina saved you."

"How?"

He nuzzled into her hand, rubbing his cheek against her palm. "Before we left their home, Amina insisted I take a wish as a boon for bringing Eshna back to her. I tried to turn her down, but she wouldn't allow it. She gave me a token, and when you were hurt, I used it to summon her."

"Amina was there?" A brief moment, a flash of turquoise eyes framed with dark hair, her whispering voice, Evin wishing for Callie to live.

Evin nodded, his brow furrowed as he continued. "She performed a miracle and was able to heal you."

Callie sensed there was more. There always was more when it came to Fae, especially based on what she had learned about them from Ianthe. Magic of that magnitude usually required something in return. "What did it cost?"

Evin paled, closing his eyes. He'd been preparing himself for this moment, the moment where she might turn him away because of the deal he'd made. She might hate the fact that they were bound.

"What did it cost, Evin?" she repeated, this time moving her hand away from his face and wrapping her fingers around his.

He took a deep breath and released it slowly. "I gave you some of my life to extend yours."

She squinted. "What does that mean?"

Of course she wouldn't accept his vague answer; he had to try to explain. "It means, *mo rua*, that we are now bound. We have a shared life force. I gave up some of my life span to extend yours."

She sucked in a sharp breath. "But why—"

"There's more. It also means if something happens and one of us dies, the other will too, fairly quickly."

Her heart stopped. "Why would you do that?"

He bent forward, resting his forehead against hers. "Because, *is tú mo ghrá*. You have my heart. I can't live without my heart, without you."

Her heart stuttered back into rhythm. She blinked staring up into his amber eyes, which glowed despite the glamour. "I love you too," she whispered. He kissed her gently, tenderly trying to convey all of his love and adoration in that one action without hurting her, and she kissed him back, diving into the sweetness of the kiss and the depth of emotion behind it.

"I was afraid you would be angry," he confessed when he pulled back.

Her eyebrows drew down, cutely creasing at the top of her nose. "Why?"

"Because being bound like that means it will extend your life beyond a natural human life span. You will outlive all of your family, and I'm not sure how it will affect your aging. The spell is old and wrapped in secrecy, so it's something we won't know for sure until later."

She brought his hand to her mouth, kissing his wrapped palm. "Then we'll figure it out together."

He sighed and smiled.

"Are there really stitches under here? Grams said something about stitches."

He chuckled. "There were, but the minute we could, I had Conall take them out and used some salve to heal the wound. I have some to use on your other wounds, too, once you're released. We wouldn't want the doctors finding your rapidly healing wounds too interesting. As it is, you may heal faster because of the blood bond. I'm not sure, but for the time being, I'm afraid you're stuck with human medicine."

There was a faint knock before Callie's mom reappeared at the door. "Visiting time is over, I'm afraid, but our patient should be home within a day or so. She tested negative for rabies, so we just need an all-clear on her wounds and we'll be set."

"Rabies?" Callie asked.

"Remember? The wolf was rabid. That's why it attacked you, *mo rua*." He winked, pressing a kiss to her temple as her mother sighed. "I'll be back as soon as they'll let me," he promised, hooking his pinky lightly around hers.

EPILOGUE

Six weeks later

"WHEN'S EVIN COMING to drive with you?" Ianthe asked, helping Callie shove some of her clothes into a box. She was due to leave for college the next day.

"Some time tonight. He said he'll be staying at Conall's."

Ianthe smirked. "But not until after sneaking over here to give you a kiss, I'm sure."

Callie's cheeks flushed. "Like Conall wouldn't do the same."

"True. I can't believe my little Callie is all grown up." Ianthe wiped a fake tear from her eye before the jacket Callie threw smacked her in the face.

"Knock it off, and don't you dare start with all the feels. Save it for when we go our separate ways tomorrow. Tonight is for celebrating, starting with some froyo!" Yesterday had been her last shift at Yogurt Land much to

Vicki's dismay, and she was looking forward to seeing her new friend one last time before she left town. Surprisingly, George had welcomed her back with open arms after her time in Fae. Ianthe and Conall had done quite the job of convincing him she needed time off to properly deal with discovering Steve's body. Vicki had been worried about her, but thankfully, Ianthe had been answering Callie's texts while Callie was away. "Will Conall be joining us?"

Ianthe smiled, her eyes taking on a dreamy look. "He said he didn't want to interrupt our sacred girl time tonight. Isn't he just the best?"

"He does know we can have 'sacred girl time' any time we want in my dreams while I'm away, right?"

Ianthe giggled, and Callie's thoughts drifted back to Evin. It had been a few weeks since she'd last seen him. When he left the hospital that night, he had to go give his final report about the quanlier to the Seelie king. He'd been waiting to make sure she was out of the woods before he left but couldn't put it off any longer. He needed to know Bronwen had been dealt with and explain certain discrete details about their new bond with the king and his dad. When he broke the news that he didn't want to fill his brother's shoes and take his father's place, to say they were both disappointed would have been putting it lightly, but they eventually came around. He still agreed to serve the king as his guard but requested time in the human realm as well, which he was thankfully granted.

Ianthe's voice broke through her thoughts. "When does Jordan get there?"

"He texted me that he arrived last night."

"And how's the whole friends thing going?"

"Good, I think. I mean he was disappointed, of course, when I told him I was getting back with my ex, and I won't deny how awkward it was running into him at the movies last weekend while I was there with Evin. It's not like Evin was subtle about things." Callie's cheeks heated remembering the way he had pushed her hair back, his fingertips grazing her neck as he whispered in her ear. "Oh, did you ever get around to asking Conall what *mo rua* means?"

Ianthe smiled mischievously. "I sure did."

"And?"

"Are you sure you want to hear it from me and not Evin?"

She nodded. Every time she tried to ask him what it meant, he would silence her with a kiss that left her breathless and unable to recall what she had asked him to begin with.

Ianthe's smile grew. "My red."

Callie cheeks turned crimson thinking about how much Evin loved her hair. She couldn't wait to see him that night and was so glad to know he was driving with her to college and helping her unpack. Even if he was only staying a few days, it was something. They were making it work, and that was what mattered. They had their whole lives ahead of them to figure the rest of it out, and from what Callie had gathered, that would be a much longer time than she had ever dreamed possible.

ACKNOWLEDGMENTS

This year and this book journey have been full of ups and downs. Thank you readers, for sticking with me through the closing of InknBeans Press after losing our beloved Boss Bean, Jo. Thank you for supporting each revision, new title, and new cover as I rereleased the series on my own. I know you all have been patiently waiting for the next book in the series, and thank you for sticking by me with nothing but kind words and encouragement. I hope it was worth the wait.

A huge thank you to my husband, Hassan. I thank you every time, but really, for putting up with my crazy, you deserve it. Thank you for always pushing me to be a better person and a better writer. I always value your advice and honesty.

It takes a lot of people to mold a book once it's written. Thank you to my beta readers: Callie Vestal, Amalia Ayers, Tonya Shaw, and Haley Wolf—you each added a little something different to this one with your much appreciated feedback. Chelsea Mueller—our writing dates were my saving grace this year. Thank you for helping me with countless blurbs, feedback, and advice. I'm so honored to call you my friend! Thank you, Murphy Rae—your covers are everything! I'm lucky to have you as my cover designer and as a friend. Caitlin—you find a way to take what I meant to say and make it sound like poetry. Thank you for your amazing editing skills! Alyssa at Uplifting Designs—you amaze me with how you take a plain document and make it look so pretty! You are truly talented, my friend. And finally Stacy Garcia—thank you for your beautiful teasers, bookmarks, and whatever else I need even when I wait until the last minute to ask.

I'd also like to acknowledge my author tribe, those who offer endless advice and encouragement when I need it the most—Teagan Hunter, Sara Ney, Manuscript Minxes, Jennifer Rebecca, Fisher Amelie, ME Carter, my other BS authors, and anyone who's allowed me to hop into their reader group and take over. I love being part of a community where we can support and promote each other. Colleen Hoover, you've always been a source of inspiration and a great friend. Thank you for allowing me to be a part of Book Bonanza as well as being part of The Bookworm Box. I can't tell you how much it meant to me to see *Fate* in the hands of so many readers thanks to the YA box.

Finally, a HUGE thank you to my family and friends: my parents, who taught me to read and love books as much as they do; my sister, Kristann, who is my number 1 table buddy; my brother, Vance; and my friends—you know who you are. You guys have always supported me in my endeavors, and it means the world to me. And to my past students—each one of you has touched my life, and I hope you achieve your dreams.

About the Author

Cathlin Shahriary lives in North Texas with her husband, cats, and dog. By day she is an elementary teacher, nurturing future book nerds and writers. By night (and weekends and school breaks) she is an avid reader, cat fosterer, and writer. You can usually find her fangirling over books, authors, and TV shows (like *Supernatural*, *Dr. Who*, and *The Walking Dead*, to name a few). She still believes in the existence of magic and the power of love.

Follow Cathlin on

Facebook: www.facebook.com/authorcshahriary

Instagram: @cshahriary

Twitter: @cshahriary

Made in the USA
Columbia, SC
05 August 2024

39476955R00159